I0835858

This Book Belongs To

dpInk
DonnaInk Publications, L.L.C.

Nocturnum's
Muse

A MONTANA RISING NOVEL

MONTANA TERROR

Serial killer madness . . .
a relentless killer harnesses the skies.

GERHARD PLENERT

United States of America

A DonnaInk Publications Imprint

A MONTANA RISING NOVEL

MONTANA TERROR

*Serial killer madness . . .
a relentless killer harnesses the skies.*

GERHARD PLENERT

Nocturnum's Muse
Publishers Since 2012
An imprint of DonnaInk Publications, L.L.C.

Library of Congress Cataloging-in-Publications Data. 2024937094
Name: Plenert, Gerhard, author.
Title: "Montana Terror" / Gerhard Plenert

Description: *"Montana Terror," is the third and final title in the "Montana Rising" mystery, suspense, and police procedural series. In this volume, Jill England is a lead investigator as Chief Inspector Reynolds assistant. She's on the clock, working hard to decide who is responsible for the series of bodies continuing to drop around her investigation. This whodunnit takes twists and turns at every path of new discovery and every time readers believe they have figured it all out – another surprise hits them. This is truly an easy to consume novel where readers remain invested in the story until the very last page.*

Identifiers: ISBN – 13 – 978-1-960431-88-2 (HRD) | 978-1-960431-38-7 (alk. paper). BISAC: FIC022060 - FICTION / Mystery & Detective / Historical; FIC022020 - FICTION / Mystery & Detective / Police Procedural; FIC022040 - FICTION / Mystery & Detective / Women Sleuths; FIC022050 - FICTION / Mystery & Detective / Collections & Anthologies.

296 p. cm.

Printed in the United States of America
First Edition: 12 11 10 9 8 7 6 5 4 3 2 1; 2024.

Book design by: dpInk Ltd. Liability Company.

For more information contact:
DonnaInk Publications, L.L.C.
17611 Aquasco Road
Annapolis, MD 20613

1390 Chain Bridge Road
#10029
McLean, VA 22101

www.donnaink.shop | donnaink@gmail.com

By Gerhard Plenert

Montana Rising Series

Montana Bleeds

Montana Scourge

Montana Terror

The History of The Small World Series

The Siege of the Small World

The Uniting of the Small World

Saving the Small World

The New Templars Series

Dawn of the New Templars

Activating the New Templars

Other Fiction Titles

The Dragon Pit

Non-fiction Business Titles

Discover Excellence: An Overview of the Shingo Model and Its Principles - Edited by Gerhard Plenert

Driving Strategy to Execution Using Lean Six Sigma: A Framework for Creating High Performance Organizations - Gerhard Plenert | Tom Cluley

Finite Capacity Scheduling: Optimizing A Constrained Supply Chain - Bill Kirchmier | Gerhard Plenert | Gregory Quinn.

International Management and Production - Gerhard Johannes Plenert, Ph.D.

International Operations Management - Gerhard Plenert

Lean Management Principles for Information Technology - Gerhard J. Plenert

Making Innovation Happen - Concept Management Through Integration - Gerhard Plenert | Shozo Hibino.

Module 17 Operations Management - Gerhard Plenert

Reinventing Lean: Introducing Lean Management into the Supply Chain - Gerhard Plenert

Strategic Continuous Process Improvement: Which Quality Tools to Use, and When to Use Them – Gerhard Plenert.

Strategic Continuous Process Improvement: Which Quality Tools to Use, and When to Use Them – Gerhard Plenert, Ph.D., CPIM

Strategic Excellence in the Architecture, Engineering, and Construction Industries - Gerhard Plenert | Joshua Plenert

Supply Chain Optimization through Segmentation and Analytics - Gerhard Plenert

The eManager: Value Chain Management in an eCommerce World - Gerhard Plenert

The Plant Operations Handbook: A Tactical Guide to Everyday Management - Gerhard J. Plenert

Toyota's Global Marketing Strategy: Innovation through Breakthrough Thinking and Kaizen - Shozo Hibino | Kolchiro Noguchi | Gerhard Plenert

World Class Manager - Gerhard Plenert, Ph.D.

This Book is dedicated to Renee Sangray Plenert
(No, she's not in the story even though she thinks so.)

And, the 8 Kids, and the yet to be Numbered Grandkids,
Who Work Hard to Bring Mystery into My Life.

TABLE OF CONTENTS

A MONTANA RISING NOVEL

MONTANA TERROR

Serial killer madness . . .
a relentless killer harnesses the skies.

GERHARD PLENERT

TABLE OF NAMES

Key Actors

The Key Players

The Key Players - in sequence of how they appear in the story:

- Gerd Plet - teenager sneaking a swim in the pool.
- Jenny Pickel - teenager sneaking a swim in the pool.
- Jill England - Lead Homicide Detective.
- Eric Falcon - Son of Roger and Judy Falcon, owners of the Falcon Sand and Gravel Company in Helena, Montana.
- Morton Mararac - the mortician and coroner.
- Brooklyn Fuller - the CSI lead.
- Kate Burkenstead - Consultant and advisor to the military.
- Commander Mark Simeon - Fort Harrison Montana Army National Guard Armory base commander.

- Matthew Christ - Lead FBI agent.
- James Planter - Vice Commander under Commander Simeon and later his replacement as Commander.
- Heidi Forengi - The new Vice Commander under Commander Planter.
- Dick Sangret - Cowboy and Kate's dance partner.
- Conner Brighton - Base Operations Commander.
- Samuel Ledger - Helena homicide detective and techie under Jill
- Hilda Bittpicker - FBI techie agent under Matthew.
- Brack Heldinger - Bad guy; later changed his last name to Hellringer.
- Conrad Toughfston - FBI replacement for Matthew Christ.
- Dereck Hardness - Kate's boss.
- Bilco - the IT techie working for Conner Brighton
- Mireille - Base housing command.
- Titus - Facilities maintenance command.
- Captain Viola Grant - Officer connected with the military base.
- Lieutenant Blanch Taylor - Officer connected with the military base.
- Crum - Boulder resident and retired police officer

A MONTANA RISING NOVEL

MONTANA TERROR

Serial killer madness . . .
a relentless killer harnesses the skies.

GERHARD PLENERT

EPIGRAPH

Anne Rand

Written in 1957 and truer than ever today.

"When you see that in order to produce, you need to obtain permission from men who produce nothing - When you see that money is flowing to those who deal, not in goods, but in favors - When you see that men get richer by graft and by pull than by work, and your laws don't protect you against them, but protect them against you - When you see corruption being rewarded and honesty becoming a self-sacrifice - You may know that your society is doomed."

Ayn Rand,
Atlas Shrugged, 1957

ONE

It was late summer. They walked hand-in-hand down the dusty back alley which ran between two stretches of houses on each side of them, each set of houses pointing out in opposite directions. The alley was used as a driveway allowing cars to park in the parking garages that were behind each of the houses. The homes on the east side of the Cathedral of Saint Helena were old, brick and mortar homes that dated back to the early settlers of Helena, Montana and they were too close together, side-by-side, to allow for cars to drive between them from the front, so the traditional carriage houses which were now converted into garages were all located at the back end of the properties and their entrance was through the back of the property.

The two knew which house they were going to. They knew the homeowners were not home. The house was one of the larger and nicer homes in the area. It was a two story, brick and rock exterior, with ivy growing over much of the outside. And, of course, they had a nice pool in the large, long backyard, just waiting for someone to take advantage of the slightly chilly water. Today was a rare warm day and it would be a shame to waste such a beautiful day when a refreshing swim followed by a lay out in the sun would be perfectly delightful. For Montanans, the slight chill of the outside air did not matter. It would be a crime to not take advantage of the opportunity for a refreshing dip in the pool.

The owners of the house were snowbirds, which was the slang name given to those people that ran away from Montana avoiding the late fall, winter, and early spring snowstorms. They headed to the lower states with their motor homes where the weather was warmer. The owners of this house had repeatedly run away each winter for the last four years and the entire neighborhood knew their routine.

Gerd and Jenny had been friends since grade school, which was how it was in this part of town. Everyone knew everyone and they knew all about each-other's lives. They weren't necessarily close; they were just nosey neighbors who kept up on each other's gossip.

The two intruders arrived at the back gate. Gerd Plet quickly climbed to the top of the fence in his attempt to jump over. Unfortunately, his shoestrings were untied, and his foot got hung up on a crack between two top boards. The momentum of his rapid climb and jump carried him over the top of the fence and he ended up face planting on the lawn on the other side of the fence. Embarrassed, he jumped up quickly and went to open the gate for Jenny. Unfortunately, he found it had a paddle lock on it.

"You're going to have to climb over the fence too," Gerd yelled. "The gate's paddle locked. I can't open it."

"You're going to have to come back over here and help lift me to the top of the fence," responded Jenny. "I can't get up there without help."

"Fine," responded Gerd, but because of his fall, he now had angry thoughts which were a lot harsher than that response sounded. He retied his shoes and worked his way back over the fence, this time being more careful not to get hung up.

Once on the other side Gerd said, "Let's do this." He cupped his hands together and held them out for Jenny to step into them.

His plan was to boost her over the fence once she was standing in his hands.

Jenny could see what he was trying to do and she put her right foot into his hands and pushed herself up so that she was standing in his hand on the one foot. Gerd started to lift her up but she wasn't completely ready. She lost her balance and fell toward him causing him to also lose balance. The two came crashing down to the ground. Jenny successfully planted her butt right in Gerd's face as they stumbled to the ground.

"That wasn't the most graceful thing we've ever done," complained Jenny as she tried to climb up off of Gerd.

"I'm just glad it was your butt and not your elbow or knee that hit me in the face," said Gerd. "At least it was something soft."

Jenny was not certain how to react to Gerd's comment so she resisted saying anything. She gave him a confused look.

The two got up, once again in position, this time a little steadier in their effort for Jenny to get on the top of the fence. She was successful even though it was still a bit of a fight for her to swing herself over the top of the fence. Once she had her body shifted so that her legs were on the inside of the fence, she pushed herself off and made a reasonably graceful drop to the ground. There were a few stumbling steps afterward, but in the end, she successfully was able to stay standing.

A few moments later Gerd was also on the yard side of the fence, brushing himself off from having landed on the ground a couple of times.

"We made it," was Gerd's comment. "Let's see if the pool is warm."

Gerd was sixteen, six foot five, and the quarterback of the local high school football team. Jenny was, of course, a five-foot ten cheer leader and the two were destined to be the homecoming king and queen.

Now that they were in the back yard, the pool was inviting them in, and they were quick to strip down and take a dive. They expected the water to be a little chilly, but they knew it would be worth it. It was fun just to try and get away with being in the pool when no one else was around. Besides, he had fantasies that he might get lucky and this was the perfect setting.

Jenny was hotter than normal in her itsy-bitsy teeny-weeny yellow polka-dot bikini, Gerd was not far behind in his racer swimming trunks. They swam around, chasing each other, grabbing and groping whenever an opportunity presented itself. Gerd could not resist the chance to untie Jenny's bikini top and she paid him back by pulling down his trunks. After their fun in the pool, they laid out on the lawn for a little sunbathing. They were quiet, just enjoying the peacefulness soaking in the sun when suddenly Gerd yelled out, "There's a drone watching us."

Gerd had spotted the remote-controlled drone flying silently in the air about twenty feet above them, its camera obviously pointing and recording them.

"Someone's spying on us," barked Gerd, pointing in the direction of the drone acting as if the yard was a private retreat where no one else had any business being there.

"How rude," complained Jenny Pickel as she wrapped a towel over herself in an act of defiance. "Can you hit it with a rock or something and knock it down?"

"I wish I had a football," he responded. "I'd be able to nail it good." He walked around looking for a rock. Finding a couple, he took aim and threw one at the drone, just nicking it on the outside edge. Unfortunately, the rock ricocheted off of one of the propellor blades and was knocked directly into the large showcase window at the back of the house, causing a small crack in the window.

Swearing, Gerd said, "That dang thing moved just as I was letting go of the rock. I'm going to take it out with my second rock. I'll finish it off for sure."

The drone did not seem seriously affected. It continued to watch them. Gerd was quickly ready with a second rock. He took aim and just as he was about to release the rock, a puff sound could be heard. Gerd collapsed to the ground and lay there, the second rock still firm in his grasp.

Jenny screamed, "Gerd! Are you okay?" She jumped up and ran over to his side. Slightly left of the center of his bare chest was a small red circle, slowly oozing blood. Jenny screamed. She had watched enough television to know she should check his pulse - his heart had stopped. The bullet must have pierced his heart and because his heart was not beating and blood was flowing out of the wound. She jumped up and ran over to her purse to get her phone. After grabbing her purse, Jenny went back over to Gerd's side dialing 9-1-1 as she ran. Standing close to Gerd's head positioned next to the pool, she held the phone to her ear and waited for the response to her call. There was another puff. Jenny fell face down into the pool still clinging to her phone. She lay, floating face down on the top of the water.

The drone slipped quietly away, heading off in the direction of the front of the house, then across the street, and then over a few more houses until it reached the location of its owner.

About fifteen minutes later, sirens could be heard blaring their resonating sound off in the distance.

TWO

The detective, Jill England, was now in a tight but comfortable relationship with Eric Falcon, son of Roger and Judy Falcon, the owners of the Falcon Sand and Gravel Company. After the murder on the Falcon cement machine, she had spent a lot of time with Eric and the two had become close. She had moved in with him and they were now living in a house on the company property, a house which had previously been the residence of Eric's grandfather. Jill had recently been promoted to the position of lead detective in the Helena homicide division. Fortunately, the homicide business had been slow since the Falcon kidnappings and murders. The last murders had been connected with the attempted kidnapping of Roger Falcon.

Jill was in her mid-twenties and had recently graduated from the university as a criminal investigator. She was a good-looking American Filipino. Both her parents had immigrated from the Philippines before she was born. She had a killer smile and a cute body. Besides her physical beauty, she had a personality that made everyone comfortable around her. Guys tended to immediately fall in love with her because of her Asian mystique, which was uncommon in Montana and her uniqueness made her a novelty.

Jill was a little distracted because of another over-the-phone fight she had had the previous day with her parents. She had become estranged from her parents who lived in New York. They could not understand why anyone would move to what they considered to be a bug and disease infested wilderness, such as Montana. They were city people. They learned to respect her abilities, but wanted her home, and considered New York . . . home. But Jill was a little on the rebellious side. The more they lectured her, the more she pushed back, and resisted their requests.

She had a happy childhood and loved her parents. But the older she became, the more she disagreed with their religious beliefs. They belonged to a church very prominent in the Philippines called Inglesia Ni Cristo. They expected Jill to follow the same teachings and would not accept the fact she was a grown woman making her own choices. Jill thought of herself as a Christian but thought Iglesias's version of Christianity was extreme. She felt Christ taught love, but this church hung onto members using fear. She did not believe that fit with Christ's teachings. Her parents insisted she was a lost soul. This became the major continuous point of contention between Jill and her parents.

After yesterday's call she felt sad because once again she had allowed them to make her angry. Jill did not want to be angry. She wanted to love them and have them love her and be proud of her. But all they seemed to see was negative. She felt she was constantly under pressure from them; like she was never good enough and had to change something to please them. No matter what she did, there would always be something wrong. She allowed these frustrations to make her feel a slight sense of depression and exasperation.

Jill was glad she had moved so far away from her parents. She was especially thrilled to now be living with someone she considered her soul mate, Eric. Additionally, she loved the beauty of Montana and freedom of living beyond her parents' reach. She also liked being free to make her own choices. She decided life was a trade-off and she still had not decided what trades she was willing to make. But for now, she was thrilled with her life, and her current situation.

Over the last years there have been a few suicides in Helena. There was the case of a wife shooting her abusive husband. None of these challenged the capabilities of detectives in Jill's department. Today, she anticipated another uneventful morning. She woke up slowly with Eric. Then received an urgent phone call from a 9-1-1 operator who said, "We received an urgent call. It sounded like someone was shot."

Jill responded with, "I am on it. Tell me what you heard. I will head out as soon as you give me a location."

The 9-1-1 operator told Jill she had heard the puff sound, and then a splash into the pool. Thankfully, the phone had a GPS tracking signal and must have been waterproof because she was able to locate the exact address of the caller. She knew something bad had happened but was not sure what the situation was so she dispatched an on-patrol officer who was close by the location of the call. He went to investigate.

Jill was off with her sirens blaring, she communicated with the officers in the patrol car, and the police radio allowed Jill to listen in on the conversation. The 9-1-1 operator explained, "All I heard was something that sounded like it might be a gunshot followed by a splash. The caller was not able to communicate with me after that. I think the caller fell into a pool because the sound on the phone went dead, but the GPS tracking system gave me the address that I relayed over to you."

"Thanks for the update," replied the patrol officer. "We will let you know what we find. We are only three minutes away."

Five minutes later, a response came from the officer on the scene, "We have two dead bodies in the backyard of this home. Both appear to be shot. No sign of a weapon or any threat. The shooter has left the scene. We need a murder detective, the CSI unit, and a coroner."

The message was relayed to Jill and the three teams, homicide, CSI, and the coroner, were immediately dispatched. About thirty minutes later all three were on the scene and a thorough investigation was started. Jill England, the recently promoted lead homicide detective for Helena Montana, studied the two bodies, attempting to make sense of what happened. "What do you think happened here?" she asked the CSI investigator, realizing it was probably too early for any conclusions to be formed.

The investigator responded, "It is too early to tell anything, but they both seem to have been shot from the direction of the house. It is going to be tough to tie this down without a weapon."

Detective England requested a search warrant, which was delivered about thirty minutes later. Then she ordered her team, "We need to break into the house and thoroughly search it for intruders or weapons."

The detectives and CSI team did as instructed and gave the house a thorough search. In the end, two handguns were found, but neither had recently been fired. The CSI team took them with for ballistics examination, but they were already convinced that it would be a waste of time.

The search inside and outside of the house gave no clues as to who the perpetrator could have been. After spending four hours going through the crime scene, the bodies were removed, and the CSI team had completed their investigation. Now the remaining work would be done by the coroner, the CSI labs, and eventually all that investigative work would be handed over to the homicide detectives so they could conduct a thorough investigation that centered on a search for the killer.

The bodies had been identified and now Jill had to perform the dreadful job of informing the parents. She knew that would be a heartbreaking experience.

THREE

The following day Jill England was in the coroner's office meeting with Morton Mararac, the mortician and coroner, and Brooklyn Fuller the CSI lead.

"What have we got?" asked Jill.

"Not much," responded Brooklyn. "We do not have a weapon. We have no sign of a break-in. The owners are snowbirds and are hiding out in Florida. They have been there for the last three weeks. They have someone checking the house once a week, which was three days ago, but they have not given anyone permission to stay in the house, or to use the pool. The kids must have jumped the fence so they could use the pool. There is nothing to indicate anyone else was there. No one was in the house and we are pretty sure the shots were not fired from inside the house."

"Unfortunately, that is not very helpful," responded Jill. "I was hoping for something useful."

Morton jumped in, "This may help. We found the bullet trajectories were from above. They came from the house side of the pool area, but they were fired from above the house. I do not mean from the roof, that is too low. The shots came from somewhere about fifteen to twenty feet above the roof of the house."

"Are you suggesting an airplane or helicopter?" asked Jill.

"They would have to be further away, and that would not be accurate enough for these shots. I say that because there were only two shots and both were direct hits," added Brooklyn. "We need to ask around but from our previous questioning of the neighbors they heard nothing like a helicopter or an airplane."

Morton added, "It had to be from a remote drone equipped with a .22 caliber weapon of some type. The bullets were .22 long rifle bullets, but they could have been shot from a pistol; however, they are not that accurate so, I am thinking it was a rifle."

Jill asked, "Let me get this straight. We are looking for a drone outfitted with a .22 caliber rifle. How does that work? How is that even possible?"

"I checked and you can get something like that on eBay," responded Morton. "There are actually dozens of options like the RMUS Heavy Duty Police Drone, which is extremely accurate. It was originally intended for farmers protecting sheep or cattle from wolves or coyotes, but from what I see here, someone has decided to use one for executions."

"And I suppose we have no way of tracking or identifying anyone who might have an outfit of that type?" asked Jill.

"We can figure out who bought them, but there is no guarantee someone from another state did not buy it and bring it to Helena. Also, it is possible to take almost any drone and add an attachment to it that includes its own remote firing mechanism. That would make it impossible to track."

Jill jumped in, "But you are sure it was a drone used in these killings?"

"Positive," responded Morton. "I do not see any other way to achieve this level of accuracy from twenty feet above the roof of this house."

"That opens up an entirely new world of crime making it super hard for me to do my job," complained Brooklyn. "How do you analyze a crime scene when there is nothing to analyze? All we have is a bullet. That is not much."

Jill responded, "This is definitely a challenge. We have two bodies, no motive, no suspect, and no weapon? This is definitely going to be challenging. Now I have to go on a drone hunt." Then she turned to Brooklyn asking, "Is there a range limit on drones?"

"That depends on the drone," responded the CSI lead. "It depends on how much money you want to spend. I personally have one and its range is a quarter mile. But they can go up to two and a half miles and even beyond that if we start looking at the military drones. They fly them in Iraq and Afghanistan, and they are based in Nevada. The type of drone we are talking about can be far enough away to where the person running the drone cannot see the drone and is relying entirely on the cameras to drive it."

"That leaves me a pretty big circle to investigate," added Jill.

"What makes it worse is, someone could be sitting in a car a couple blocks or even a mile away from the crime scene and fly the drone in, do the murders, and drive off without having any kind of residence within the two-and-a-half-mile radius," added Morton.

"Thanks for the bad news," added Jill. Then, turning to her detective companions she added, "Let's start searching for anything within a radius of a half mile out and work ourselves out from there. We will worry about the drive-by option if we get past the two-and-a-half-mile radius." Jill furthered . . . "Everyone in the neighborhood seemed to know the teenagers that were killed. Apparently, they are celebrities in the area because the male was a local football superstar and the girl was a local prom queen. We used pictures and talked to several lookie-loos in front of the house. They all gave us the same names. We have already shared the bad news with their families. So now, the search for the murderer goes into full swing."

"What are we looking for," asked one of the detectives.

The senior detective responded, "Ask each house if they have a drone and if they answer 'yes' ask if you can take a look at it. If they say, 'no you can't see it' then all we can do is make a note of the location and possibly get a search warrant if we feel it is worth a closer look. The other thing we need to do is to ask if anyone has seen a drone in the air during the time of the shooting. It is a long shot but it would be stupid if we missed something obvious like that. The third thing we can do is see if there are any surveillance CCTV cameras in any of these homes or small businesses, which may have picked up a drone flying around during the time of the shooting. A lot of homes have security cameras. They might have picked up something. If we can get a drone on camera in the area during the time of the shooting, then we will know our search is heading in the right direction. We may have something to work with."

"Sounds boring but we are on it," responded the detective.

The CSI lead said, "If you can get a picture of the drone, even if it is a fuzzy one, it will give us something to look for. We can probably identify the type and then search for recent purchases of that type of drone. We would love to have anything we can dig into. There is nothing to work with right now."

"What else can we do? Are there any other ideas you can think of? Are we missing any obvious holes in our search?" asked Jill of everyone in the room. "I think we are forced to do the boring and routine house-to-house canvas of the area working at half mile intervals from the crime scene. Let's get started."

"We just do not have anything else to go on," responded Brooklyn.

There were no other comments. No one had any additional suggestions that might help in the investigation. Jill ended the meeting, frustrated there was so little to work with but convinced they were working on the only appropriate plan.

FOUR

He drove into a neighborhood on the northwest side of Helena near the Lewis and Clark County Fairgrounds and parked his blue Toyota Tundra four-door pickup. He parked in a secluded area of the parking lot, minimizing the chance of anyone seeing him. Then he prepared himself for his day's work.

He was a meticulous planner and had spent weeks preparing for this assignment. He had acquired the correct tool for the job, which in this case was a remote-controlled police drone outfitted with cameras and a rifle. Then he travelled to Helena and started the execution of his plan. At night he took the extra precaution of parking the pickup in a two-car sized garage storage unit, which he had rented for this operation. Occasionally he slept on the back seat of this pickup, but every second or third day he would take the drone out of the pickup and get a hotel room by driving to a nearby hotel so he could take a decent shower.

The two-car garage also allowed him the privacy he needed when he needed to work on the drone, which included loading its twenty-two-caliber rifle, cleaning the propellers, and greasing the gearing. It also allowed him to do some repairs, like the time he crashed the drone into a high-power line shorting out some of its circuitry. Those repairs turned out to be more extensive and caused him some delays in the execution of his plans. On longer drives, like to a hotel, or to a restaurant, he would leave the drone in the garage. The garage had become the perfect hiding place for the work he had to do.

Today he had driven to an area where there was no one around. He wanted isolation. He didn't want anyone to see what he was doing. The drone was in the back of the pickup on the bed. It was large for drones, about four feet diameter and hexagonal in shape. He pulled the tarp off the machine which had conveniently kept it hidden until he was ready to use it. He hit the switch and the six drone motors started whirling. Then, using the remote, he lifted the drone slowly and carefully off the bed of the truck. After it was above the truck bed, he allowed it to jump straight up into the air. Soon it was at a sufficient altitude, about one hundred feet up, allowing its driver to move around the neighborhood and scope out his next target.

The drone moved swiftly and quietly, about one hundred feet above the ground. It would drop down to forty or fifty feet if a closer look was needed. The drone was a special model, designed for stealth, and unless you saw it, you wouldn't know it was there because it moved so quietly.

This neighborhood had larger and newer homes than the old town neighborhood where he had been just three days earlier. There were no swimming pools to be found, but that was okay because there were plenty of people to choose from out in their back yards with their barbeques. Besides, he didn't need a lot of targets, one or two was sufficient for his purposes. He flew over Northgate and soon found himself an elderly couple, out in their backyard, lounging in their chairs as they watched their steaks getting cooked. "These steaks will be perfect," the chef told himself.

Their house was one of the larger ones in the neighborhood. It was stucco with decorative lava rocks on the face. In the back was a large pergola which offered a little shade. The couple were lounging under the shade, relaxing and chatting with each other. The couple seemed comfortable and were enjoying their retirement years. Little did they know what was in store for them.

The drone's driver waited until the husband, in his sixties, six foot tall and bald, was flipping the stakes on the barby and then he shot him from behind, high and to the left side of his back and right through the heart. The man fell on top of the barbeque, knocking it over and falling on top of it. The wife, also in her sixties, a short five foot five with grey hair, screamed and ran over to see what had happened and just as she was leaning down, trying to pull him off the barbeque, she was hit in the center of the back of her neck. She fell on top of him and they both lay there, his skin roasting away and starting to smell of burnt flesh.

The drone, having done its damage, also included a homing app which allowed its owner to just push a button and the drone flew back, settling itself back onto the bed of the pickup. With the drone settled in, its driver pulled the tarp back over the top of it and secured it. Then he started up the pickup and drove off, feeling successful with himself at having completed another assignment. Now that he had created these diversions, he was ready to execute the real mission that he had been given. .

As he drove away, he mumbled, "Fifty-two and fifty-three."

FIVE

The neighbor, smelling an unusual smell, which stank of burnt flesh, at first didn't want to be rude. Eventually the smell became so strong he could no longer resist and peeked over the fence. He was shocked when he saw his two neighbors crumpled over a fallen barbeque. He yelled out to them, receiving no response. He knew this wasn't right and rushed around the fence line to their back yard gate. He opened the gate and ran to the aid of his neighbor, but it was obviously too late. He pulled the wife off the husband, and then pulled the husband off the barbeque in the hope of stopping the burning of his flesh, but the damage had been done. They were both dead.

The neighbor screamed at his wife to call 9-1-1 and get the police to the scene. She asked, "What's the problem?"

He responded, "They're both dead. They've been killed. I see bullet holes in both of them."

She quickly made the call and ten minutes later a police cruiser could be heard shrieking its siren in their direction. Once on the scene the police rushed into the backyard where the neighbor and his wife were now standing. "What happened here?" one of the two arriving officers asked.

"I smelled the burning flesh of the husband, peeked over the fence, and saw him laying on top of the barbeque," the neighbor responded. "His wife was lying on top of him. I pulled her off of him and then pulled him off of the barbeque so that his flesh would stop burning. They were both dead, both looked like they were shot from behind."

"We'll need to get statements from both of you," responded the one officer while the other called for a coroner, a CSI team, and a homicide detective to come to the crime scene.

About thirty minutes later the three teams arrived. As usual the CSI agents were the first on the scene and they went to work analyzing the bodies and the area surrounding the murders.

"You shouldn't have moved the bodies," complained Brooklyn, the CSI detective scolding the neighbor who had come to the rescue.

"I couldn't just keep them cooking on the hot fire?" responded the irritated neighbor. "That would be stupid."

"Tell me exactly how you found them," commanded the detective.

"The husband was lying over the top of the barbeque, as you can tell by the burn marks on his clothes and body. There was a bullet hole on the back side of him, which must have caused him to fall. The wife was lying on top of him. My guess is that she came over to check on him when she was also shot in the back, again causing her to fall on top of him. That's how I found them. He was lying directly over the barbeque, and she was laying crossways over the top of him. I pulled her off, checking to see if there was a pulse or any breathing, and there was none. Then I pulled him off because he was creating a strong smell. He was still cooking over the coals, as you can tell by his burnt flesh."

"They are both lying face up," responded the CSI detective. "You must have rolled them over in the process."

"Of course. I didn't lift them off, I just rolled them off. They're too heavy to lift!"

"How did you know there were bullet holes?" asked Brooklyn.

"I'm guessing that's what they are because I don't know what else they could be," responded the neighbor. "There are small pin-holes on the back of both of them. Roll them over and take a look."

At this point Jill had arrived and was listening in on the conversation. "I just wish you had left everything alone," complained Brooklyn.

Jill jumped in and said, "I'm sorry Brooklyn but I think the neighbor did the only logical thing he could do. He was concerned about his neighbor, not about your data collection. And if they had still been alive, he might have saved them with his actions."

Brooklyn grumbled something indistinguishable under her breath and continued her work photographing and documenting the crime scene. Jill turned to the neighbor and instructed, "We'll need to debrief you and write up a report on what happened here. I'll have one of my detectives work with you to get it written up."

"Sure," responded the neighbor, "But I'm not really sure what happened here. I can only tell you about my part and that was pretty much after the fact."

"Do you have any idea how long they had been lying here?" she asked.

"Not really," responded the neighbor. "I started smelling something strange a couple hours ago but didn't connect it to them burning themselves up until the smell became really bad. Then I looked over the fence about an hour ago and found them like this. I really don't know any more. They must have been shot at least two hours ago, and probably a little more."

"Thanks," responded Jill. Then she took both neighbors out to the street to one of the police cruisers and introduced them to the detective which would be taking their statements and writing them out for signatures.

Jill returned to the crime scene to find that Brooklyn and the coroner had rolled the bodies over so they could check the bullet holes. She asked, "Did you learn anything?"

The coroner responded, "I think you may have a serial killer here. These bullet holes look like they came from the sky as well, not from any shooter on the ground. I need to go back to the lab to make sure, but I'm suspecting that you have the same shooter with the same weapon. We won't know for sure until Brooklyn does the ballistics comparison, but it looks like a .22 bullet shot from a drone. If it's the same gun, that would convince me that you have a serial killer to deal with."

"Keep me updated and let me know as soon as you know anything," responded Jill.

"You bet," responded both Brooklyn and Morton at the same time, causing all three to snicker.

SIX

The following day Jill was in the coroner's office where she was meeting with Morton and Brooklyn. "What do you have? Why did you call me down here?" Jill asked.

"We have confirmed both sets of murders were performed by the same weapon," said the CSI investigator. "We have s serial killer in our midst."

"Who have you told this to?" challenged Jill.

"No one," responded Brooklyn. "We wanted to let you know first so you can decide next steps."

"Let's keep this out of the newspapers until I have confirmation from the Chief of Police and the DA on how they want to proceed," instructed Jill. "We don't want to create a panic just yet."

"Understood," responded Morton.

Brooklyn spoke up, "There's more. One of your detectives was able to come up with several homeowner's videos from the first shooting. Most of them didn't record much since they were primarily pointed toward movement on the ground and didn't register any movement in the air. But there was one that did capture a picture of the drone. It wasn't very close so it's a bit fuzzy, but at the very least we now know for sure that the executions were preformed using a drone. We have a description of it, and a picture of it, but no identifying names or numbers because of the fuzziness."

"Wow," responded Jill. "That's great. Let me see the pictures."

Brooklyn pushed a picture of the camera shot, and a picture of a similar drone taken off the internet, over to Jill to look at.

"Excellent work," Jill said. "Now we know we're on the right track."

Brooklyn continued, "From this we know the direction that the drone travelled, and we are now searching for more home cameras in that direction."

"That's really great work," responded Jill. "You've made great progress. Keep up the good work. I'm going to report to Chief Farlow as soon as we're done here. Is there any other helpful news that you've discovered?"

Both Brooklyn and Morton shook their heads, "No!" and Jill stood up to leave. Then Brooklyn added, "We're doing the same search for CCTV recordings at the latest murder scene and hopefully we'll find more videos."

"Perfect," responded Jill as she left the meeting and went directly to the Chief of Police. Knocking on his door she heard him say, "Enter!"

She entered the room and closed the door behind her. Then she went to the chair opposite his desk and sat down. "We have a big problem," Jill started to explain. "Apparently, we have a serial killer. Both sets of recent murders were performed using the same weapon, and it appears that the weapon is being wielded by a drone. It appears the drone must be really quiet since no one seems to hear it, but we know it has to be a drone because of the angle of the bullet trajectory. Normally I can't confirm trajectory until I have completed the autopsy, but I brought along a knitting needle this time because I suspected it to be the same type of shooting." She held up the needle to show those around her what she was using. Then she continued her explanation, "There's nothing up from the direction from where the shots are being fired but blue sky. But we have found a home video showing the drone in motion about the time of the shootings and we're using this information to try to track down the drone. We're also looking for other homes that might have had a home security video camera installed which might give us better resolution on the drone. It would be great if we could come up with some identifying marks or numbers. What is concerning is that there seems to be no connection between the two sets of murders. They seem to be totally random."

Chief Farlow said, "It looks like your team has done a really good job of getting your arms around this. The idea of a serial killer raises all kinds of concerns. It means that we need to bring in the State Police and even the FBI. I know you don't like that idea, but it's a federal requirement that we get all the help possible in situations like this. Continue doing your good work, and I'll talk to the DA about the next steps. Hopefully, your team knows to keep this out of the papers?"

"I've made a point of telling them exactly that, but we've had leak issues before," responded Jill. "I'll do my best to keep it under wraps for as long as possible."

"Excellent," said the Chief. "I'll call the DA as soon as you leave and let you know what the plan is as soon as we have one."

"Thanks," said Jill as she stood up and left the office. She went back to her own work area where her team of homicide detectives were deeply involved in working on the details of the investigation.

The homicide detectives had an unusual arrangement for their office. It was all in one room with desks surrounding the walls on three sides of the room. Jill's desk was in the middle of the room along with a large conference table. At one end of the room was a wall where she would call the team together and update them on everything that she had learned during her meeting with the mortician, the coroner, and the Chief. She ended her update by stressing the importance of not creating a panic by leaking the possibility of a serial killer.

Then Jill assigned a couple of detectives to work with the CSI team in chasing down the region around the latest murders to see if there were any home videos of the drone.

After the update she asked her team if they had any additional information or ideas that would help in solving the case. One of the agents asked, "Is there a way to use radar to track drones? Maybe the airport has a way to track them and maybe they already have information that can help us."

Jill responded with, "That's an excellent idea. Will you follow that up for us and check with the military at the same time to see what they have available that might help."

Her team was familiar with the drill. They had made excellent progress in figuring out how the murders were executed, but they still didn't have any suspects, any weapon, or any motive. They were a long way from getting these murders wrapped up.

SEVEN

"Montana? Why on earth would you want me to go to Helena, Montana? They have guns there! Lots of them! Isn't there another place where we could go to do this?" She was flabbergasted. This assignment could have been carried out anywhere. Why Montana of all places?

Kate Burkenstead was five foot six, red hair, and she looked like, walked, and talked like a fireball who was in charge of any situation. It felt like her bright green eyes could penetrate anyone right to the soul. She was often referred to as Merinda, the Disney princess from the movie Brave, because her hair was so curly. Her nickname on her last project was "scary canary" and it fit her perfectly. But in spite of the criticisms, she was always successful in accomplishing her assignment.

"Listen Kate," responded Dereck Hardness, her boss and the caller on the other end of the line. "It's not your choice. It's your job. And the person hiring us wants this done in Montana because the commander there has a special interest in solving this problem. He's convinced that the mole is somewhere within his command, which is in Helena to be specific. Get yourself there as quickly as possible, understood?"

Dereck was the primary interface between the US government and/or large private sector businesses and arranges the connection with the contracted agents that work for him. He arranges the contracts, negotiates the terms including timing and cost, and then assigns one of his agents to carry out the contract. He has had previous government connections, including his having achieved the rank of General in the Air Force, which gave him high level government visibility, not just in the USA but in numerous other countries. Leadership in government and private sector businesses were very familiar with his work and know about the capabilities of his agents, who were also mostly retired military. Dereck's business operates very much like a consulting company, but without the public identity and visibility that normally goes along with a consulting company of this type. Many of the projects or contracts were "off the books" because the individuals making the contract prefer anonymity.

"Got it," Kate replied. "But this is stupid." Kate was a contractor who performed odd strategic manipulation jobs that no one else wanted, and she was good at it. She would often find herself in hot water about something that someone had gotten her into, but she was used to that. One of her strangest assignments was guarding the cattle from attacking Kodiak bears for a cattle rancher on Kodiak Island while he was away travelling.

Kate had a long history of rebellion. She never knew her parents, having been dropped off at a hospital when she was a baby. From there she went through the child protective services system her entire life, always the temporary resident of numerous foster homes. She was never anyone's permanent family member. She was always considered to be an outsider.

When she was a teenager, bouncing between numerous schools, she was bullied. During several of her teenage years she found herself in a foster home on a reservation. This was especially tough because being one of the non-Indians living on a reservation opened her up for a large amount of discrimination. But she considered bullying as an asset because it taught her to be tough. She learned how to fight for everything she wanted and that gave her an attitude where she mistrusted everyone. At one point she joined the military, with the fantasy of becoming a Navy Seal, but her stubbornness and lack of discipline became her enemy and she left the Navy after one term of duty. She could see the writing on the wall that she was never going to be a Seal.

While in the Navy she came across an investigative unit, which piqued her interest. She worked with them off and on, on the side, and became very interested in developing her career as an investigator. One of the men she was working with, Dereck Hardness, was on the verge of retiring from the military, and he asked her if she would be interested in working for him as an investigator. He saw her stubbornness and her ability to work on her own as an advantage. The relationship and bond had been created, and that's where Kate ended up working for many years up until the time of this assignment.

She was often used in assuring compliance or investigating fraud during elections or searching for moles in police departments. This time wouldn't be any different. The Army National Guard in Helena was convinced that they had a foreign spy in their midst, and they needed an outside specialist with no ties inside the military to weed out the perpetrator. That was the assignment she had now taken on, and it worried her because of the size of the organization and because the assignment could involve foreign terrorists and international intrigue.

She punched in Expedia.com and checked on flights into Montana. There was nothing that went to Helena which didn't include a couple of layovers, and she hated layovers. But this was a job and she hadn't had a good posting for several months, so she decided to go ahead and grab it.

She booked a flight which hubbed through Salt Lake City and ended up in Helena. From there she caught an Uber to the Fort Harrison Montana Army National Guard Armory office. She went to the Commander's office and informed the secretary there that she was expected and to let him know that she had arrived.

The secretary made a quick call, confirming the visit from Kate, and then led her into Commander Mark Simeon's office. The commander was a stern looking man, six foot five inches tall, dark hair and engrossing green eyes. His mere presence commanded the attention of anyone visiting him, and Kate was no exception.

The commander started the conversation with, "Welcome! Have a seat. We have a lot to talk about. I'm not exactly sure where to begin or how much detail you want so I'm going to let you ask questions."

"Why don't we start with the question, 'Why do you think you have a spy? What led you to that conclusion?'"

"Information leakage," was the commander's response. "We, talking about the United States and primarily the agents of the CIA, have our own spies overseas, and when they come back telling us stuff that we thought was secret within our organizations then we know we have a problem. At this point we're sending out misinformation and using this spy to misdirect what other countries think they know about us, and that part has worked because we see their responses to our misdirects. We tried to use misinformation as a trap to identify the spy, but that hasn't worked. That's why you are here. We've been searching for this informant for a couple years now and still don't feel like we're any closer."

"I'll need access to everyone and everything,"

"To do that we'll need to confirm your clearance level," responded the commander.

"Let's get that done because I want to start attending all meetings at all levels and I need that to start immediately. I'll need to be informed of all meetings. The other thing I'll need is access to all leadership for a thirty-minute one-on-one interview with each of them. I'll also need a staffing list of everyone in the command."

"Once you're verified none of that should be a problem."

"Let's take care of that right now," Kate suggested. "Call your commander right now and let's get that approved so I can get the information I need to press forward."

The call was made. Approval was given. And Kate was given the information she needed to move her investigation forward.

Kate continued, "One more thing; next time you give out false information, can you give it out differently for different groups. It might work that we can localize the false information to a specific group."

"That's an excellent idea," responded Commander Simeon. "I'll make a plan to send that information out immediately and we'll see what, if anything, we learn."

Kate scheduled meetings with each of the leaderships, setting up one hour with each individually over the next couple days. She also received a list of all the meetings that were scheduled over the next week so she could observe the behavior of the attendees to the respective meetings. She would present herself as a human resources specialist that studied the staffing needs of the guard so that everyone felt comfortable with her presence in the meetings. Then she would use the staffing list to slowly study and analyze the behaviors and reactions of everyone present.

EIGHT

Commander Mark Simeon would arrive on base from his off-base housing at six AM and often stay until seven PM. He liked being the first one in and the last one to leave. He felt that set a strong example for the remainder of the troops. He wanted to present a strong work ethic for everyone else to follow.

After his long day of meetings and losing about half of the day prepping materials for Kate's investigation, he was exhausted and delighted that the day was finally finished. He had planted a series of misdirect messages, hoping that Kate's idea about narrowing down the search would actually work.

The drive home was a short fifteen minutes. He was hoping for a barbeque tonight, but the two couples who were recently murdered in their back yards had sent fear throughout Helena causing everyone to avoid backyard activities. Nobody was willing to spend any time in their back yards for fear that another drone shooter would strike. Somehow the message that these killings were done by drone had leaked out to the press. The entire idea of a drone being used as a murder weapon sent chills throughout. Several random private drones had been shot out of the sky by shotguns as a result of the newly created fear. As yet, none of the downed drones had weapons attached. Everyone who owned a drone was now afraid to fly their drones for fear that they were going to get shot down.

But the drone used in these murders was very quiet and unless you saw it you wouldn't know it was there. And its driver knew his target and knew how to get close to it. This time there was a definite target, not just some random hit. This time the killer knew what had to be accomplished and he was convinced he would be able to meet his goal.

Thoughts of the drone complicated the commander's mind as he drove home. He felt that there had to be more to this than just a couple of random shootings. They were too similar to each other to be completely off the cuff and random. There had to be a stronger motivation for these attacks. They had to be coordinated in some way. There had to be a bigger plan behind it all. This caused him to wonder if the investigations that were occurring on the base had anything to do with the shootings. "Of course not," he said to himself as he drove along. "That wouldn't make sense."

Commander Simeon shifted his thoughts to the various assignments that were made during the meetings that occurred throughout the day. He was happy that Kate was there to do the investigation, but he could see that she would also put an extensive demand on his organization's resources. However, he knew that this investigation in search of the mole within his organization was something that needed to be done, and the sooner the better.

He approached his house and drove up in the driveway, parking there rather than in the garage because the garage was too full of junk to fit the car. He parked the car and put on the brake, opened the door, and stepped out of the vehicle. His sixteen-year-old daughter came running out of the house to greet him, but what she really wanted was to use the car later that evening. "Hi dad. How was your day?" she asked.

"Super busy, but I survived," was his reply.

Then there were two puffs. One hit him on the back of the neck and the other hit his daughter in the center of the chest. They both fell to the ground, immediately dead. A neighbor next door who was just coming out of his house to climb into his own car saw them fall and immediately looked toward the sky. He saw the drone and quickly slipped down next to his own car and away from the drone, hoping the drone wasn't going to be shooting at him. He pulled out his smart phone and started to take rapid-fire pictures of the drone as it turned and started to pull away. Once the drone was too far away for pictures, he used his phone to call 9-1-1 and report what had just happened.

Just then the commander's wife came running out of the house screaming. She ran directly to the two family members, screaming her head off when she realized they were both dead.

Ten minutes later the patrol police arrived and thirty minutes later the homicide detective, the CSI detectives, the coroner, and the military police were on the scene. The homicide detective Jill England was confronted by the neighbor who told her he had taken pictures of the drone. She immediately confiscated the neighbor's phone with the comment, "This will prove to be invaluable. This is the biggest break we've had yet. Thanks for taking the risk to take these photos."

"Do you mean all these drone murders are connected? That they were all done by the same individual?"

Jill realized she had just leaked a vital piece of information, that this was a serial killer, so she tried to backtrack, "Actually, what I mean is this is the best information we've had in any of the cases, but we have no idea if they are connected. That's something we are trying to figure out."

Unfortunately, standing within earshot of the conversation was a news reporter who didn't miss the comment. The headline for the evening news would read, "Local police believe that the drone killer is a serial killer!"

NINE

Brooklyn Fuller, the CSI lead, went to work on the photos and video recorded from the commander's neighbor. It was an excellent video, better than expected. "These new smart phones have incredible cameras," she commented to her assistant. It wasn't long before they had excellent pictures of the drone, including the sticker identifying its brand and model number. Unfortunately, the serial number had been covered over so identifying the owner of this specific drone would not be easy.

The next step would be to go to the manufacturer and find out how many drones of this model were sold and to whom. With that information the CSI team could hit the phones and see how many of the drones were accounted for and which would have unknown locations. It would be a long and tedious search, but they knew how critical it was to identify this killer and put a stop to this stream of murders.

"I hope they didn't make too many of these drones," commented Brooklyn to her CSI team. "I need everyone to take a break from what you're doing and hit the phones. We need answers as soon as possible."

The drone manufacturer was more than willing to supply as much information as possible. They didn't want their drones to be labelled as a murder weapon. They feared the repercussions of the bad publicity. "We have produced 2,100 of that model," responded the marketing manager of the production company. "Four hundred are still in stock which leaves 1,700 out there in the hands of retailers or customers. Unfortunately, we don't have all the names of our customers, only those that registered for a warranty. I can get you those easily enough. But the rest you're going to have to get from the retailers themselves. I can get you the retailers and the number of units sold to each. That's about as much information as I have."

"Please send it to us ASAP," responded Brooklyn. "We need to nail this killer before he does any more damage."

Jill, who was in the CSI office at the time Brooklyn made her plea, suggested, "I'll try to get you some phone support from other units as well."

"That would be wonderful," responded Brooklyn. "We need to bag this guy."

Then Jill added, "Unfortunately, since we now suspect a serial killer, we're going to have to bring in the FBI and they're going to charge in here and start bossing us around. Let's get as much done as we can before that nightmare begins."

"Understood," replied Brooklyn.

Jill made a call to her old FBI contact Matthew Christ. "We suspect the possibility of a serial killer," Jill informed him. He already knew about the murders, but a formal request was needed before he could step in.

"I'll be there in the morning to investigate and if I agree with you, we'll be charging in there in full force," commented Matthew.

"See you in the morning," commented Jill.

At Jill's request, the entire homicide team joined the CSI team on the phones. They went late into the evening, making calls to customers of the drone. Nobody on either team wanted to go home. They all desperately wanted to catch this killer, and they wanted to do it right away.

It was nine in the evening when some of the officers started drifting out of the police station and began heading home. So far, they have been able to eliminate and tie down about three hundred drone units. There were still a lot of phone calls that needed to be made.

The morning was a continuation of the previous night. Lots of phone calls needed to be made. The Police Chief sent additional staff to join the team in their barrage of phone calls. By noon, another three hundred drone units had been located. From these calls they were able to identify half a dozen units that seemed to be missing in action and required further investigation. The local police in each of the areas that had jurisdiction over each of the missing units were dispatched to locate and identify the location of their drone. The team felt that they had made excellent progress and they hoped that soon the rogue drone unit would be identified.

Also, around noon, Matthew Christ, the FBI agent, arrived at the Helena police headquarters. It was a pleasant reunion for him and Jill, who had worked closely together on the series of Falcon murders. "I see you're back at it here in Helena chasing another killer," was his opening comment.

"Happy to see you too," was Jill's blunt response. She admired Matthew, but he was a little scary too. He was the spitting image of one of Hitler's superior race Nazis. He had blue eyes, blond hair, and a six foot two look that was so admired by the Arians. But his personality was as far away from the white supremist mentality as anyone could possibly get.

Matthew enjoyed working with Jill. She had her quirks, but she was dedicated to her work, and she knew how to do her job.

"Update me on what's going on here and why you think you have a serial killer on your hands," requested Matthew.

Jill gave him an update on the three pairs of murders, all with the same MO (Method of Operation) and the same ballistics. "It's too coincidental to be anything but a serial," she added. "Ballistics tell us it was the same weapon that was used in each of the murders. What we can't find is any connection between the three crime scenes. The victims seem totally random. The only thing they have in common is that the crimes occur outside, in the yard, which is obviously because you can't get the drones inside a building. We had a bit of luck at the last crime scene in that a neighbor took a series of pictures and videos of the drone. We've identified the manufacturer and have the model number and we are going through an extensive search to find the owner of the drone. Unfortunately, the serial number has been overlaid by a sticker so we couldn't get that information, but what we have so far has significantly helped us reduce the search. So far, we have half a dozen possibilities, but nothing firm." Jill showed him the pictures of the drone that had been plastered on their crime scene wall. She also showed him the pictures of the three crime scenes.

"Excellent progress," confirmed Matthew. "If you have any delays in the investigation or in the search for those unidentified drones, we can send an FBI agent out there to help check it out."

"Then you agree that we have a serial here?" questioned Jill,

"You had me convinced when you told me you had a ballistics match from the three crime scenes," agreed Matthew. "I'll get the FBI on it and of course we will take over the investigation. But you have given us an impressive foundation to start with."

TEN

Kate was about halfway through her interviews at the Helena military base when she received the news that Commander Simeon and his daughter had been assassinated by someone the news media had labelled as the "Drone Killer." About an hour later, when she was in the middle of another of her interviews, she received a message informing her that Vice Commander (VC) James Planter wanted to meet with her immediately.

As Kate arrived at the Vice Commander's office, she was immediately escorted into his office. "Have a seat," ordered VC Planter.

"What can I do for you Vice Commander?" asked Kate.

"It's no longer VC. I have been promoted to Depot Commander. What you can do for me is stop wasting my staff's time with your interviews and leave the base immediately."

Kate was taken aback, and it took her a couple minutes to recover. Then she asked, "Is there a problem with what I am doing?"

"Your presence here is a problem," he responded. "You make everyone nervous and they're gossiping about what's going on and what you're finding. You have everyone wasting a lot of time in this witch hunt and I need them to be productive."

"I'm following the directions given me by Commander Simeon," she responded. "He's convinced that you have a mole in your command, and he was desperate to have it rooted out."

"Enough," responded Commander Planter. "You're done here. Leave the base immediately and don't take anything with you that you collected while you were here."

"This is quite unusual," responded Kate. "I'm not accustomed to being fired like this for no reason."

"It is what it is. That's how we roll," responded the commander as he waved her out the door.

Kate followed orders, but she didn't give up. She immediately contacted the contractor who had given her this assignment and reported, "I have been kicked off the Army National Guard base here in Helena. Apparently, after the commander was killed, the vice commander saw no need for my services and thinks I'm just keeping his staff from doing more important work. He ordered me to leave the base immediately. What do you want me to do?"

"Stay in Helena while I make a call to the Pentagon and ask them about next steps. They may want you to continue your investigation at a different base. Or they may have a chat with the new Commander to make sure he supports what you're doing. Stay put and I'll get back to you when I receive further direction."

Kate took advantage of the day off and played tourist. She went to the Cathedral and visited a few museums. She also strolled around Helena's 'Old Town'. Having still not heard anything from her employer, she decided to visit a couple of ghost towns outside of Helena.

While she was driving in the hills around Helena, she had lost the signal. She didn't realize there weren't cell towers everywhere. This was a new experience for her. That would never have happened in New York. When she eventually realized her phone wasn't working, she turned and headed back toward Helena. As she came into the range of one of the cell towers, she realized she had received a phone message from her boss. The message said, "The Pentagon wants you back on the Helena base in the morning. They will be communicating with Commander Planter sometime today and will be informing him this is a priority for them. You will not be working with the Commander, rather you will be working with the new Vice Commander, Heidi Forengi who is arriving on the base later today. She will be coming from a base in North Dakota and has already been briefed. Her primary assignment is to facilitate your investigation. My understanding is that because she is being transferred, she will only be on the base from ten AM till noon, so you must catch her during that time. Get back to me if you have any questions."

A smile came over Kate's face. Not only would this be a blow to Commander Planter's ego, but it would mean all the work Kate had done up to now would not be a waste of time. She would now be able to continue her interviews unhindered. She also wanted to learn if any of the false messaging Commander Simeon had given out had been received through the spy network. She wanted to know where the leakage was occurring, and hopefully be able to tie down the division that was the source of the leak. With the support of the new Vice Commander, and especially with the backing of the Pentagon, her job just became a lot easier.

For now, she was going to find herself a buffalo burger, and then spend the evening in a cowboy bar hoping to do a little line dancing. One of her previous assignments had her in Austin, Texas for six months. She was at the cowboy bars country dancing every chance she could get. She became obsessed with it. And she hoped to find the same type of entertainment in Helena. She heard from the attendant at hotel registration that the Windbag Saloon and Grill was the place to go but she wasn't sure if they had dancing. She intended to check it out and if it fell short of her expectations she had a couple of other places, like Miller's Crossing, she would have to check out.

She found herself in the bar which gave her both the buffalo burger and the dancing. She knew she didn't have to rush on base in the morning since the VC wouldn't be there until ten and she would probably be given a hassle if she arrived any earlier so she didn't plan to arrive before ten. She decided to have a little fun tonight.

Maybe it was the third drink, or maybe it wasn't, but she agreed to dance with a stud of a cowboy who was teaching in Carroll College's Anthrozoology degree program. He hailed from Augusta, Montana and was a good dancer, so they circled the floor several times doing the two step. It was the third time around the dance floor before she learned his name was Dick Sangret. They spent the rest of the evening together. Fortunately, he was a gentleman and didn't ruin what had been a very enjoyable evening by asking Kate to come to his apartment for the night.

Dick did ask her to meet him again at the same bar the following Saturday. "My favorite band will be here on Saturday and I'd love to reserve a table for the two of us. Hopefully, we can get in a little more dancing."

"I'd love it," responded Kate. "I'll see you Saturday."

It was midnight when the two left the bar, each heading toward their own vehicles. Then Kate returned to her room at the Holiday Inn Express and went directly to bed. All the dancing had been more of a workout than she was used to, especially so late into the evening. She was asleep in minutes.

Kate was slow to get up the following morning. She woke up at eight and slowly got ready for the day. She grabbed the free scrambled egg and sausage breakfast and left the hotel around nine-thirty. Her CAC card got her on the base and she drove over to the Vice Commander's office where she sat in the lobby waiting for Vice Commander Heidi Forengi to arrive. The VC arrived five minutes early and asked Kate to follow her into her office. "I received instruction from the Pentagon I needed to give you my full attention and support," the VC informed Kate. "I've read the brief on the mole hunt you are conducting and I understand the level of security required. You and I will need to stay in constant communication. We will be the only ones that know the details of the investigation."

"What about Commander Planter?" asked Kate.

"He knows this investigation is ongoing, but he will not be involved in the details," responded the VC. "That's the way the Pentagon wants us to proceed."

"Excellent," responded Kate. "Then I can continue my interviews as previously planned?"

"Yes," responded the VC.

"What about the bogus information that Commander Simeon distributed?" asked Kate. "Have we had any of that come back?"

"As a matter of fact, yes! We have seen some information filtering through." The VC handed a document to Kate which informed them about specific information that had been retrieved in North Korea.

"This is excellent," responded Kate. "It gives me some direction. I'll follow up on it right away."

"What direction does it give you?" asked VC Forengi.

"It tells me the leak is somewhere in the leadership of this base and not in the non-commissioned workforce or in the civilian workforce," responded Kate. "It narrows the search down considerably."

"I'm impressed!" responded the VC. "You've already reduced the search considerably and you've only been at it a few days."

"Thanks, but we still have a long way to go," responded Kate. "Now I'm going to go out and rearrange the interviews that were cancelled on me. I need to continue my search for your mole."

"Good luck," was the VCs comment as Kate stood up and left the room.

ELEVEN

He was shocked when he saw the newspaper report about a 'Drone Serial Killer' which included a picture of his drone. There were a few swearwords that came flying out of his mouth. He knew what he needed to do. He needed one more pair of murders to keep everyone confused, and then he needed to ditch the drone.

"We're in luck," he said out loud to himself. "It's the Fourth of July and there will be lots of people out celebrating. I can do this in the dark. Lots of people will be out and no one will be looking for a drone in the dark."

Time passed slowly and he was extremely nervous about executing this last pair of murders since everyone in the city would now be watching out for him and his drone. He hoped to finish his mission at around ten in the evening, but this time of year in Helena it was still bright enough to see. It would be another hour before it would be dark enough to complete his mission.

At about ten-thirty, the fireworks kicked in. He found himself in a suburban housing area in the north side of the city where there were minimal fireworks. Nothing much was shooting up into the sky. The fireworks that he saw were mostly on ground level, which would make it more difficult to spot the drone.

He parked his truck at the end of a road that was completely dark, fired up the drone, and watched it lift off out of the back of the pickup. At this point it was plenty dark and he grew confident that this mission would be easier than he had previously anticipated. He felt silly that he had spent the day stressing out for nothing.

He went high with the drone just in case he encountered any stray fireworks being shot up in the air. Most of the collections of people doing fireworks included families and he didn't want to shoot two individuals from amongst a large collection of people. Eventually he found the perfect target. It was an elderly couple sitting out on the street in their lawn chairs watching everybody else's fireworks.

He positioned the drone so that it would be partially hidden behind the roof of a house across the street from the target. Then he fired, but this time the sound of the shot was drowned out by fireworks noise, and no one noticed. The old man slumped down in his chair which apparently was normal for him because his wife didn't seem to notice. Then the second shot was fired, and the elderly lady slowly slumped down and continued falling forwards until she fell out of her chair.

He saw that his mission had been completed and he raised the drone high up in the air, away from the fireworks and the noise. He knew what he had to do next. He had to ditch the drone and he had already decided that the best place to ditch it would be in one of the many lakes along the Missouri River. The lakes that were a short distance northeast of Helena, like Hauser Lake, weren't desirable because they were too close and they would most likely be the first place the police would look. He decided to use the north end of Holter Lake, a large lake north of the Gates of the Mountains, one of the many scenic tourist areas along the Missouri.

He kept the drone in the air while he drove his pickup to Interstate 15 and started driving north. He was concerned about the range of the drone and didn't want it falling out of the sky before it had reached its destination. He flew the drone about halfway to his desired ditching location and let it hover in the air while he drove to Spring Gulch where there was a convenient exit off the Interstate on to Recreation Road. From there he continued flying the drone the remainder of the way to Alligator Point, a curved deep-water area of Holter Lake.

The drone only had two hours of battery life and so far, he had drained at least half of that. He flew the drone over to the base of the head of 'Sleeping Giant,' one of the mountain formations in the area which was clearly visible from Helena. He parked the drone on the bald head of the giant and decided to wait for about an hour until he was sure the fireworks had finished.

After a while he flew the drone high enough to allow him to observe the activities along that portion of the lake. Unfortunately, the deep area where he had anticipated ditching the drone was still heavy with fireworks. The lake was surrounded around the outside edge by boats, all observing the fireworks. In the middle was a pontoon which was being used as the base for shooting off the arial fireworks.

He held the drone up in the air, off to the south end of the lake above the trees, watching and waiting for the arial fireworks to end, but they seemed to go on forever. "They're doing better fireworks here on the lake than they did in Helena," he grumbled out loud to himself. He parked the drone on one of the bald rock outcropping that was free of any trees or brush and he let it sit there while he waited.

He started the blue Toyota Tundra pickup and drove over to a different pullout along the road. He didn't want to raise suspicion by staying in the same place too long. He parked, shut off the truck lights, and waited. He picked up his cell phone and played his favorite game for a while.

One hour later he lifted the drone up off its hiding place and flew it back to the deepest section of Holter lake by Alligator Point.

The arial fireworks from the center of the lake had finished off but the boats around the outside of the lake were still there, shooting off their small, local displays for the kids. There was the occasional boat crossing the lake, but it was now pretty dark, and he felt comfortable that he wouldn't be spotted ditching the drone. When there was no one in the center of the lake he made a dive with the drone. He lost control of the drone when it was just a few feet above the water because of the mountains that surrounded the lake, which obviously blocked his signal, but he knew the drone had completed its mission and would now sink slowly to the bottom of the lake. Ironically, the location he had selected for dropping the drone was directly out in front of the cabin owned by the Falcons and which had played an important role in solving that earlier series of murders.

He started the pickup and slowly drove off, heading back to Helena. He exited at the Custer Avenue exit, driving by Lowes and, after wiping it for fingerprints, tossing the drone's controller into one of the garbage bins behind Lowes. The mission he had been tasked with was now completed, and he had earned his two-million-dollar retainer. His next step would be to get out of town and as far away from Helena and from Montana as possible. He returned to the I-15 freeway and sped off to the south for about one hour until he arrived at Butte, then he headed east on Interstate 90.

As he drove away, he mumbled, "Fifty-six and fifty-seven."

A short time earlier: "9-1-1 What is your emergency?" the operator asked.

"No emergency," responded the caller. "We have a neighborhood watch in our area and there's a pickup with Colorado plates has been parked in our cul-de-sac for about one hour. No one got in or out of the pickup. It's just parked there and I wanted to report it."

The operator asked, "Did you see anything, like a drone lifting up off the bed of the pickup?"

"Nothing like that," responded the caller. "I'm looking at it right now from a second story window and I don't see anything in the bed. It looks like there is one lone driver sitting in the vehicle and that's it. He's just sitting there."

"Thanks for reporting it. We are on a close watch for any strange activity right now so you did the right thing by calling in. Can you take a picture of it, hopefully getting a picture of the license plate?"

"I'll give it a try. Oh, wait. The pickup just started up and is starting to pull away. I'll try to take a picture."

The phone went dead, followed by a text message from the 9-1-1 operator giving the caller a place to send the picture but the picture was blurry, and it was of the side of the pickup. It wasn't very helpful.

"Just another suspicious neighbor," mumbled the 9-1-1 operator to herself. "These Montanans see a conspiracy behind every tree. It's just a pickup. Probably a couple kids fooling around, hoping they don't get caught. I'm going to report this as a 'low priority, no follow-up needed' call."

TWELVE

The police search for the drone in the night sky continued with full intensity when Jill received a call from a 9-1-1 operator saying, “We have another double homicide. No one saw or heard a drone, but with the fireworks going that was no surprise.” The operator gave Jill the address and she immediately relayed the message to Matthew. Jill and Matthew left immediately for the crime scene, followed by the several additional FBI agents, the coroner, and the CSI unit. They arrived at the scene twenty minutes later and went to work investigating what had happened. Matthew directed several of his agents to start doing interviews of the surrounding neighbors, none of which turned out to be very helpful. No one had seen anything until the lady fell out of her chair and that’s when they called 9-1-1. They weren’t even sure what had happened to her until they realized that her husband had also been shot and then they made the connection that this was another drone murder.

“This is crazy,” commented Matthew to Jill. “No murder weapon. No apparent motive. Just two random people shot as they were watching fireworks. How do we stop this guy? How do we catch this guy?"

"That's why you're here," commented Jill sarcastically. "You have got the big guns. Good luck."

The coroner and CSI agents came over to Jill and Matthew and the coroner summed up their initial findings by saying, "Looks like the same thing. It's the same caliber weapon and shot from the air. My initial read of this crime scene would be the drone killer has struck again."

"Thanks," responded Matthew. Then, turning to Jill, he asked, "Where do we stand with the phone calls?"

"We're about two-thirds through the list," responded Jill. "We have given you the eight remaining unidentified drones that need further investigation. That's all we have found so far and we feel fortunate there are only that many. What has your team learned about those eight?"

"We've sent agents out on all eight," responded Matthew. "We have confirmed five but the remaining three are challenging. Two of them are claimed to be stolen. One was from South Dakota and the other from Colorado. We're working with the local police in each area to see if we can track down the thieves. There seems to be some doubt they were actually stollen because these drones are quite large. It's not something you can easily pick up and walk off with. You have to have a pickup to haul this type of drone. But, at this point, we haven't confirmed anything for sure."

"Excellent," responded Jill. "My team is still working to finalize their screening of the sold units."

"In the meantime, how about you and I go out to dinner?" asked Matthew.

Jill could read he was after more than just dinner so she responded, "I have a boyfriend waiting dinner for me already and it wouldn't be respectful for me to bail on his dinner and go to yours." There wasn't any dinner waiting for her, but she didn't want to start something with Matthew when she had already made a commitment to Eric.

"How about tomorrow?" He tried again. "It's strictly business. We can spend time talking about the case."

"No thanks," responded Jill. "I enjoy my evening escapes from work. It's the only time off that I get."

Matthew was persistent, "Then let's not talk about work."

Jill looked down, knowing she was going to make Matthew mad, but she shook her head "NO."

Matthew, slightly frustrated by the refusal, said, "You can't blame a guy for trying!" Then he turned and walked off throwing his arms up in the air.

Jill knew this would unfortunately make working with Matthew a little more challenging. But she wasn't about to let him intimidate her into something she knew she would end up regretting. She believed in commitments. She was loyal to Eric, even if an all-powerful FBI agent was going to try his best to make her feel obligated in some way.

Jill's work at the crime scene was finished. The FBI would now be doing all the interviews and any additional investigative work. What needed to be done by her homicide team, by CSI and by the coroner at the scene, had been completed and it was time for her to go home.

On her way home, she wondered if she should tell Eric about Matthew's passes. She knew he would be bugged, but it wouldn't be right not to tell him. In the end she hoped he would be proud of her for standing up to him.

She decided to go ahead and tell Eric about Mathew. When she arrived home, she decided to immediately bite the bullet and she went directly to him and said, "I hate telling you this, but Matthew made a pass it me today, and I turned him down. Now I think he's going to be mad at me, which will make it more difficult to work with him."

Eric wrapped his arms around her and said, "Thanks for making your life more difficult just to be loyal to me. I'm a little jealous, but you're a pretty lady and I understand why other men would have an interest in you. But thanks for sticking with me. I know

I'm probably no match for an FBI detective, but I'll do the best I can to make you happy."

"I choose you," was all Jill could think of saying. And that was all Eric needed to hear.

THIRTEEN

As Friday evening rolled around, Kate was ready to spend a relaxing weekend. Weekends on the base were nonproductive because the leadership vanished. They kept their weekends to themselves and tried to avoid the base unless absolutely necessary.

Kate felt successful. She had tied the mole down to being someone in the leadership of the base. And she considered that to be a significant discovery. Now the job became more difficult because she would have to access all the communication from every leadership member in order to see which of these individuals might be behind the information leak. That would require spending a large amount of time digging and scratching for information.

But this weekend the mole search wasn't the first thing on her mind. She already knew what steps she had to do next at work. The process was somewhat routine. But what she was looking forward to now was her Saturday night dance club meeting with Dick Sangret. It wasn't Dick specifically she was excited about. He was cute enough, but she didn't know enough about him to be enamored by him. She appreciated his invitation to listen to his band and she respected him for being a gentleman and for not just seeing her as a pickup. For her, the thrill was in Western dancing that she cherished. She loved the line dances and the two step, and she knew there would be plenty of both.

She went out to lunch at the Taco Treat, which had become her favorite fast-food joint in Helena. They had something they called an Enchatreato on their menu which was a burrito smoothered, or rather swimming, in sauce, and she had already become a big fan of them, eating one or sometimes two of them a day.

She spent the day Saturday going through a few of her notes and through the communications information she had collected so far from the leadership at the base. As badly as she wanted to avoid work, it constantly nagged at her and her thoughts continued to go back to the research she was performing on the base leadership. There was occasional communication, which didn't make a lot of sense, and sounded like coded messages, but those were rare and were probably innocent enough. She was looking for a pattern. If the communication occurred regularly, to the same individuals, and always seemed like a coded message, then she knew there was more to the messages and they were probably not innocent. She found a couple incidents where the message stream seemed questionable, and she would need to confront the sender in order to get an explanation about these message streams. One was from the base Commander Planter and another was from Operations Commander Conner Brighton, a direct subordinate of Planter. She went to their calendars and booked meetings with each of them for Monday morning.

In the end, most of her day was spent on data searches. She was ready for her long-awaited night out on the town. She went early because her mouth was watering for another of those buffalo burgers that she had enjoyed on her last visit. At around eight PM the band showed up and started to set up for their gig. She didn't pay much attention to them, but rather sat back and read a book, "Dawn of the New Templars," she had brought along. She wanted to keep the table she was sitting at for the remainder of the evening so she ordered fried pickles as an appetizer waiting for Dick to arrive. She had the waiter refresh her drink, and then she sat back and read.

As the time approached eight-forty-five the band started their tune-up routine, making sure all the various pieces of equipment were in tune and operating properly. It started to look like it was going to be a fun night of music and dancing, and she was right where she wanted to be.

As the time approached nine PM Dick came to her table and sat down across from her. "I saw you sitting here and wanted to see if you wanted to come over to my table, right next to the band."

"Sure," Kate responded as she grabbed her book, her appetizers, and her drink, got up, and followed Dick to a table that was set up for the band members whenever they had a break. "You're sitting at the band's table?" asked Kate.

"That's because I'm the lead guitarist," responded Dick. "And I do some of the vocals. Let me introduce you to the band members."

"I can see why this is your favorite band," said Kate.

Dick proceeded to introduce the remainder of the band, who were also sitting at the table. "Guy's, she loves to dance so whenever your off stage, she would welcome a whirl around the floor." Just as he was finishing his introductions he said, "Looks like it's time to get to work."

The band members stood up and relocated themselves on stage with their respective pieces of equipment. Then, with Dick's count of, "One, two, three," the band proceeded to play their first set.

Kate had mixed feelings. She was delighted to know the lead singer and guitarist, but she also wanted to dance, and she couldn't dance with a band member who was busy playing music. But it wasn't long before the problem corrected itself. The band members took turns taking breaks during the set, and one-by-one as they came to the table, they took Kate out for a spin.

Kate loved the attention. She loved the mix of dancers and found out she loved the band as well. Dick's band had just jumped to the top of her list of favorite cowboy bands. They sounded a lot like Little Big Town, a band she enjoyed a lot.

In the end, Kate was delighted to have been there for the evening. For the most part, the band members were a fun bunch of guys who loved country music and loved to dance. After their second set, when they were all sitting around the table, Kate asked, “How often do you guys get together to play?”

Dick responded, “We play twice a week, once on Friday at a different bar in Butte, and then on Saturday here. Would you like to join us again sometime?”

“I’d love it,” responded Kate. “I may even be able to join you some Friday night in Butte if I get off early enough. Let me know where you’re playing and I’ll try to make it whenever I can.”

They gave her directions and she said, “I look forward to it. I think I’ve become one of your groupies.”

“You’re the only one,” responded another of the band members. “We tend to avoid the young, high school crowd because they get weird. And that unfortunately includes most of the college girls too. We all teach at the college and work together, but we’re all from different departments. This is our relaxing break from the kids. We like having you join us because you’re not out to hustle one of us. You’re just out to have a fun night and that’s what we like too. You’re welcome anytime. And you’re a good dancer too which makes it even more fun.”

Kate’s curiosity was aroused and she asked, “What areas do you guys teach in?” It turned out that in the remainder of the band there was a Mechanical Engineer, a Business Statistics Professor, and an Economics Professor. “What a strange mix,” commented Kate.

At the end of the evening, they all said their goodbyes and went their separate ways. Once again Dick was the gentleman, escorting Kate to her car, but not making any demands or overtures. “Thanks for an incredibly fun night,” said Kate.

“You’re welcome. The band enjoyed you being there. It made it more fun for them as well. You’re welcome anytime.”

Kate drove back to her hotel. It was now one in the morning and she was completely drained. She fell asleep before her head hit the pillow.

The next day, Sunday, she didn't wake up until nine AM. She hadn't set an alarm clock because she intentionally wanted to sleep in. When she finally got up, she got dressed for church, which the internet told her was at ten. It was only two blocks away and she would get there in plenty of time.

Church ran for two hours. At noon she went to the Taco Treat and got herself another Enchatreato for lunch. Back at the hotel she rested and watched television. She blew off the rest of the day and spent a restless afternoon.

It was now four in the afternoon. She wasn't in the mood to go out and do anything. She was still a little tired from the previous night so she proceeded to watch a second movie. She pulled out some of the snacks she had picked up at Walmart a couple days earlier, and she made that work for her dinner. She was just planning to blow off the rest of the day and the evening.

She spent a restless night, wondering how best to approach the questions she had for the commander. In the end, she decided to just ask him directly about the confusing communications. It didn't seem to make any sense for her to beat around the bush about it. She needed to act like she was in control of the situation and not allow him to intimidate her.

She arrived on the base at seven on Monday morning. That was the normal start time for activities on the base and she knew the commander would be there even though her meeting with him wasn't scheduled until eight. She proceeded directly to his office and waited in the lobby, hoping that he might bring her in earlier. This meeting was something she wanted to get over with regardless of if the results were good or bad.

The commander had arrived in his office ahead of her. She could hear his voice on the phone whenever the door to his office was opened by his secretary. She realized she wasn't going to get into his office any earlier than the scheduled time, so she waited.

When eight rolled around he was still on the phone and it wasn't until about eight-fifteen when she was finally invited into Commander Planter's office. "What do you want?" demanded the commander. "You realize you're just a thorn in my side and your investigation is causing my staff to be extremely inefficient. So don't waste a lot of my time here. Get to the point and let's get this over with."

Kate was expecting this type of response. Their last conversation hadn't left them on the best of terms. "There are several messages coming out of your office that don't make sense. They read like they're encrypted and they're always back and forth to the same individual? Can you explain what's going on here?"

Kate passed him the sheets with the printed messages so he could see what she was talking about.

"See! This is what I'm talking about. It's this kind of waste of time that is frustrating to me. These messages are coded and encrypted between me and one of my good buddies. We were deployed together in Afghanistan, and we just continued to communicate this way because it's fun. There's nothing secret about the messages. Just military banter."

"Then you won't mind sharing the codes with me so I can read the messages," Kate requested. "And I'll need to know who the recipient of the messages is."

"No problem, but you'll find that there is a lot of foul language and sexual innuendoes in the messages so cover your ears when you read them," insisted the commander.

"No problem," responded Kate, thrilled that the commander was going to be cooperative. "Just doing my job."

"Of course," responded the commander. "I'll message the code structure to you and the contact information of my buddy. Are we done here?"

"Yes," responded Kate as she stood up and started to leave the office.

"Thanks for getting directly to the point," added the commander as she left.

Kate proceeded to her second meeting with Operations Commander (OC) Conner Brighton. This meeting wasn't until nine-thirty, and she was going to be forty-five minutes early. Again, she decided to just wait in the lobby outside his office until the time of the meeting.

When the OC was finally available, Kate entered his office and sat down. "What can I do for you, lovely lady?" asked the commander.

Kate immediately decided that this guy was a sexist pig, hitting on her without even knowing anything about her. He was all about looks. "I have some messages that were sent by you and I don't know who these messages were to, or what they were about. They're encrypted and I need to be able to read them."

Again, Kate passed the printed messages to the OC and he looked them over. "These are just messages that I sent to a military buddy of mine. We have a little network of deployed troops who returned from Afghanistan and that's how we communicate. Commander Planter is one of the groups as well and you'll see messages like this from him."

"I need your encryption codes and I need to know who you are messaging," demanded Kate.

"Of course," responded the OC. "I'll get that to you right away pretty lady."

"Thanks," responded Kate who couldn't get out of this guy's office quick enough.

Realizing that these encrypted messages were leading her nowhere, she decided to report to VC Heidi Forengi on what she had discovered and where her investigation was going.

She went directly to the VC's office and requested a meeting. The VC invited her in immediately and Kate gave her an update on her progress.

Kate reported, "At this point we know the mole is one of about twenty individuals. I still have to get access to a lot of communications data and then analyze it. I'm not sure that's going to answer any questions, but it has to be done."

"Thanks for the update," responded the VC. "Excellent progress. Please keep me posted on any new discoveries."

"Will do," responded Kate as she left the VC's office.

FOURTEEN

Jill started the day by receiving the cold shoulder treatment from Matthew, but she wasn't going to give in to his intimidation tactics. This type of behavior always frustrated her. In her mind it was definitely classified as sexual harassment because she felt he was trying to get her to capitulate to his desires, but how would she prove it? It would just be her word against his, which led to nothing.

This was the day they were finally going to wrap up the initial phone calls attempting to trace the whereabouts of all the drones. They expected to be done around noon, at which point the police would turn over all their findings to the FBI who would in turn get all the credit for the effort. Then the FBI would check out any missing leads.

Jill and Matthew's team had been out to investigate the most recent pair of Fourth of July murders, but there was nothing new. The ballistics came back a match to the other murders, so there was no longer any question whether this was a serial killer. But the motive and the weapon still had a lot of mystery attached to them. There was no commonalty amongst the various killings other than the way they were killed. The drone, as it was manufactured, was not naturally equipped to carry weaponry, including the scope needed in order to have the same level of accuracy that a sharpshooter would need for these long-distance shots. Attaching a weapon wasn't the problem. It was capable of doing that. But which weapon was used and how it was connected wasn't clear. There was confusion as to what weapon was used and how it was attached to the drone.

As noon rolled around, the first wave of calls on the drones were finished and Jill went over to give Matthew's FBI team their findings. They had taken over the conference room and when she entered the room everyone went strangely quiet. "Here's what's left of the phone call chases," Jill informed them. "There are thirty-two missing and unidentified drones. We've already given you a dozen of them and here's the rest."

"Can't you tie it down a little better than thirty-two," barked Matthew in a defiant tone of voice.

"We've had the entire department on hold getting it to this point," responded Jill. "You're going to claim credit for the results anyway, so now you can get to work sending field agents out to see if you can narrow down the last remaining thirty-two. Good luck." Since no one reached out to receive the list, Jill dropped the list on the conference table, turned, and left the room. She was irritated by Matthew's arrogance and superiority.

"Wait," Matthew commanded.

Jill turned around and asked, "What do you need from us lowly local cops?" Then she waited.

"Anything new from the CSI team or the coroner?" asked Matthew.

"Same ballistics as the other three pairs of murders. Same trajectory. And still nothing in common with any of the other killings," explained Jill. "So basically, nothing new."

"Forward the report to me," commanded Matthew.

"You can access the reports yourself," responded Jill. "You have the same access to them that I have. What have you learned from the interviews of the neighbors? Are there any additional videos of the drone? Any more drone sightings? Anybody seen where it came from or where it landed?"

"That information is on a need-to-know basis," responded Matthew.

"That's an interesting way to say you don't know anything new. So, you have no additional information either," responded Jill. Again, she turned around and started to leave the conference room. This time no one attempted to stop her. "That arrogant idiot," she mumbled as the door closed behind her. As far as she was concerned, this case was now the FBI's and her local unit had already gone above and beyond in tying down the owners of the drones.

Jill returned to her unit and complemented them on their excellent work. "Now this case belongs to the FBI. You've all gone above and beyond and have made a big difference. Thank you." She dismissed all the volunteers who were not from her team so they could return to their normal jobs. Once they had departed, she turned to her homicide team and said, "The FBI is being secretive. They are cutting us out of this investigation. But this is Helena and we care about our citizens, so we're going to keep looking. We don't want any more murders on our streets. Do any of you have any suggestions?"

Samuel Ledger, one of Jill's rising star detectives, commented, "As you know, I'm a minor techie and love to play with new technology. I went to the airport and also talked with the local military, but their radar tracking equipment wouldn't pick up something as small as a drone. But I didn't give up there. For the last few days, I have been playing with a radar tracking tool that I assembled. I have been using it to watch the air traffic around Helena. What I have is home grown and isn't very sophisticated, but I decided to home in on the frequencies that could be used by the drone that we are searching for now that we know the make and model."

Jill's mouth dropped open and she excitedly said, "Oh my gosh, are you kidding me? Tell me what you've found."

"I think I was following one of the drones that we're talking about and I saw it fly north over the mountains. It may have come from the neighborhood of the latest set of shootings, but I didn't start tracking it right away. I picked it up when it was heading north and I lost signal when it passed over the sleeping giant, but I kept watching, hoping to see it come back, but it never came back."

"Oh my gosh, you're a genius. From this minute forward, your job is to spend all day and all night looking for that drone. You have to call me immediately if and when you see it again." Jill was flabbergasted. Why hadn't anyone else thought of tracking the drone this way? This was pure genius.

Then Jill searched the room and asked, "Are there any other incredibly brilliant ideas that I should know about?"

There were no responses. Jill proceeded to say, "I'm going to get the news media off my back and tell them we have completed the initial search for the owner of the drone. But I don't want Samuel's genius leaked. It may just be the way we will finally catch this guy."

"Understood," responded several of the homicide team members and the rest nodded their heads in agreement.

"I'm also going to share Samuel's findings with the FBI because I'm legally required to. Good work all of you. Let me know anything the minute you learn it!" Jill turned and left the homicide department and headed back to the FBI's conference room. She couldn't wait to tell them how brilliant her team was.

Jill burst into the conference room, and again the room immediately went silent. Then Matthew spoke up, "Knock before you come in here."

"Oh," responded Jill. "I forgot how important you guys are. Anyway, I have an additional update to share with you."

"Proceed," responded a grumpy Matthew.

Jill explained Samuel's tracking mechanism and told the FBI team that he would be continuing the tracking process. She told them that the drone had flown off to the north and then the signal was lost. She let them know that if Samuel discovered any additional signals from the drone, she would let the FBI know.

"We need immediate access to that equipment, and we need to take charge of the tracking process," demanded Matthew.

"It's his personal equipment," responded Jill. "You have no authority to confiscate his equipment. He's doing this out of the goodness of his heart, and it's a significant asset to the team. There's no way you can touch his equipment. In fact, I'll warn him that you have threatened to take his equipment and I know how he's going to react to trespassers."

"Is that a threat?" demanded Matthew.

"If you guys are such genesis, why didn't you think of this and do it yourself rather than demanding to confiscate someone's personal equipment. You are the one with the threat. I'm trying to offer you a friendly warning," Jill responded and she turned toward the door and stormed out of the conference room.

"Wait," commanded Matthew but this time Jill ignored his demand and continued on to her office.

Jill's next task was to call a press conference, two hours from now, where she would share the information that her team had collected about identifying the owner of the rogue drone. She didn't want Matthew to claim credit where it wasn't deserved. The war between her and Matthew was now full blow.

FIFTEEN

He had taken a detour through Yellowstone Park heading south toward Jackson Hole, Wyoming. He had finished his assignment and nothing new had come up, so he thought he would take it easy and take a slow trip on his way back home to Colorado. He decided to take the scenic route. He had no phone connectivity during most of this trip which meant that he didn't receive any text or email messages for about the last twenty-four hours. When he finally started to get close to Jackson Hole his phone beeped several times. He noticed a message from the individual who had hired him for his last assignment, and it read, "Last operation an excellent success. Don't stop what you're doing. We have another assignment similar to the last one and it would be good to confuse the two together. Stay where you are and continue what you've been doing over the last couple weeks for a few more weeks. We'll send you the new assignment in the usual way. Your fee will be the same."

"Now I've destroyed the drone and the gun. I don't even have the remote anymore. How am I supposed to continue the series of murders, and have them all be linked together, if the ballistics don't match up?"

He pulled over at a scenic pull-out. He had to think. Does he attempt to retrieve the old weapon and the drone? Or just the weapon since he has very little chance of retrieving the remote? Does he go back to Lowes and see if the bins have been emptied? And, if retrieving the drone and the weapon does not work out, how does he build another weaponized drone quickly? It can't be done and he'll have to change the weapon that he was using. That would add a layer of complication to the entire assignment.

He sent a response to the number requesting his services, "Understood. Proceed with the identification. I'll keep you posted on progress as usual."

He decided that retrieving the controller was the first challenge and if that doesn't work out then he's stuck with coming up with a new drone, or at the very least, a new weapon like a hunting rifle with a good scope. Unfortunately, having to come up with a new drone or changing weapons would mean a gap of time between this new set of murders and the last murders, which would be longer than normal. It would show some indecisiveness. Additionally, buying a new weapon meant finding a black-market source for the weapon so that he wouldn't have to go through the required background checks. False IDs might be caught during one of these checks, which was also dangerous. Another weapon might be a lead for detectives that he didn't like giving them.

He spun his Toyota pickup around and started working his way back to Helena. Then he had another thought. There are no hotels between here and Montana. He spun the pickup around a second time and drove into Jackson Hole. He parked on the side of the road and used his smart phone to search for hotels that had rooms available. Finding one, he used his phone's GPS to locate the hotel and five minutes later he was in the hotel's lobby requesting a room for the night.

The following morning, he started the long drive back to Helena, following a faster route that went up the west side of Yellowstone Park and eventually connected back with Interstate 15. This new route would only take five and a half hours whereas the previous route through the parks had taken two hours longer. He was angry and frustrated. Ditching the murder weapon was the correct and necessary thing that he needed to do. But now it seemed like the wrong thing. But how would he have been able to predict that they were going to come up with a contract that would be a follow-on to the previous murders?

The entire time driving back to Helena his mind was in a spin. He hoped that the drone's controller was still in the Lowes' dumpster. It was a specialized controller which allowed him to fly the drone, sight in the target, and shoot. It would be challenging to rebuild that controller, especially with the quick turn-around that he needed. He had built the controller himself, and he could, of course, build another, but timing was critical, and he had to get another weaponized drone into the air quickly or it would blow its MO. It would interfere with his mantra as a random serial killer.

He drove a little faster than he should have, and only stopped for gas. The trip took most of the day, and he arrived into Helena in the middle of the afternoon. While in route he had booked the Holiday Inn Express and they were waiting a room for him when he arrived.

After checking into the hotel, he had something he needed to do first. He waited until it was dark. Lowes was closed and nobody was around so he made his way around back and headed for the dumpsters. Unfortunately, there were four of them, and he couldn't remember which dumpster was the one he had thrown the controller into. Fortunately, the dumpsters didn't look like they had been emptied recently, so he took a guess. He started with the second dumpster and, using the light of the security cameras that surrounded the store, he started dumpster diving. He would yank things out of the dumpster and throw them out on the ground. It was a slow and tedious process, and occasionally he would encounter something wet and slimy, which made the job even grosser. But he was on a mission that seemed critical to him and to the mission he had now committed to.

The first dumpster yielded nothing so he moved on to the second dumpster. After sifting through the contents of the second dumpster, and making an enormous mess, he was frustrated and disgusted. He had found nothing. He moved on to the third dumpster and once again started the same process. He was about two-thirds of the way through the dumpster, throwing everything out on the driveway, when he found it. He was able to retrieve the drone controller. But not all was well. Apparently, something heavy had been thrown on top of it and one of the levers had been broken off. Additionally, something slimy had been poured on top of the controller and it was now questionable whether it would even function. He casually tossed the controller into the back of the pickup and started to crawl out of the dumpster when two cop cars with sirens blaring arrived on the scene.

"What are you doing?" came over the loudspeaker of one of the cars.

He had to do some quick thinking to keep himself from getting arrested, so he said, "I threw a box into one of these dumpsters and didn't realize that my wedding ring was in the box until just a little while ago so I came back hoping to retrieve the box and find my ring?"

"You made quite a mess here," responded the cop. "I hope you're planning to clean it up again."

"Of course," he lied. But now he realized that he had been on camera the whole time and he decided he had better clean it up or they might be looking for him. He didn't need the police looking for him over something as stupid as making a mess. If he cleaned up the mess, it would probably be the end of this.

"Did you find your ring?" asked the cop.

"Yep," he responded, holding up his left hand and showing a ring on his finger.

"Good enough," responded the cop. "Get to work on the cleanup. We'll be back in a little while to check on you."

"Thanks," he said, planning to rush the clean-up process and get out of there before the cops returned.

He went to work cleaning up the mess he had made, including the slimy gross stuff that he had encountered. He knew the cops had his license plate and would probably be checking on his registration. He had recovered the remote, but was it worth the trouble? Was it workable? Or was this entire exercise a waste of time? It was hard telling until he had the drone to test it against.

After the cleanup he went directly to his hotel and went to his room. He retrieved the controller and his toolbox from the back of the pickup, wrapping the controller in a blanket so it couldn't be identified on the hotel cameras. Once in his room he unwrapped the controller and went to work opening it up to see if it was recoverable.

The broken lever would be a problem. It's not the type of thing they had in the local hardware store or hobby shop. It would have to be special ordered off the internet. He decided he would be forced to jerry-rig something that would allow him to use the lever. He decided on drilling a small hole in the middle of the lever and then to insert a long screw, which was run into the lever base. Then the screw would have to serve as the replacement lever.

He cleared the grime out of the unit and dried it thoroughly. He was now ready to give it a try, so he powered it up. It seemed to work. The screen jumped to life, showing what the drone would be seeing, and the targeting and weapons systems seemed to be working as well.

He felt he had a working controller. Unfortunately, the next step would be even tougher. He would have to scuba dive one hundred feet to the bottom of Holter Lake and attempt to retrieve the drone. Fortunately, that was still within the one hundred thirty feet limit that most scuba divers would be willing to risk. So, the first question he asked himself out loud was, "Does anyone rent scuba equipment in Helena, Montana?" But he had an even bigger problem, which was that he hated scuba and snorkeling. He had an unreasonably enormous fear of the water which dated back to when he was about ten years old and his friends pushed him into a fast-moving river and he nearly drowned. But it wasn't like he could hire someone to go down into the lake and retrieve his murder weapon. It was something he would have to do on his own. And it terrified him.

His night wasn't very restful. He kept waking up wondering and worrying about how he was going to sync these two assignments together. In the end he may not be able to find the drone or get the weapon working. He may have to build an entirely new weapon, or maybe even resort to using a rifle. But that would disconnect these new murders from the old murders, and that's not what his customer wanted. For now, he was going to have to go for a swim.

The following day he did an internet search for scuba equipment in Helena and he found an outfit that was connected with the local university that gave scuba lessons. That would be perfect for what he needed. He contacted them and asked if he could rent their equipment for a day.

"For a day," asked the individual on the phone. "What is there to do around here that would require scuba equipment for just one day?"

"A small boat sank in Holter Lake and some important keys and equipment sank with it," he responded. "I'm going to attempt to retrieve those items and maybe the boat as well if I can tie some ropes to it."

"Good enough," was the response. The story seemed believeable enough. Then the attendant provided their hours and location information.

"I'll be right over," was his response and the phone line was disconnected.

He did exactly that. He went to the supplier of the snorkeling equipment, picked up what he needed, and headed north on Interstate 15 to Wolf Creek, which was the closest access point to where the drone was dumped. He drove up the road to the lake and parked at the Boat Loft, where he proceeded to rent a boat for the day. Then he took off across the lake.

The drive to the area close by Alligator Point where he had ditched the drone took about fifteen minutes. It was in an area where there was no connectivity for his phone and where the outside rim of the lake was lined with cabins that were only accessible by boat. They were mostly deserted during the week. Nearly all the activity on this part of the lake was on weekends.

He wasn't exactly sure where to look. He knew where he had lost contact with the drone, but he doubted that it sank straight down. It most likely drifted along with the flow of the Missouri River which fed the lake. The river continued on after the dam.

When he was close to where he felt the drone would be he donned his scuba equipment and dove in, realizing that this was one of the deepest points in the lake. He descended lower and lower, trying desperately to maintain mental control. In spite of all the conversations he was having with himself, he was slowly starting to freak out.

He eventually made it to the bottom of the lake. Then he started to zig zag back and forth continuing along with the flow of the river. He moved along quite a distance and having seen nothing, decided to work his way back upstream and a little over from where he had searched for the first time. He spent about the same amount of time on his return, assuming that the amount of time he spent swimming would also give him the distance of his swim, but he again saw nothing. Moving over a little more, he followed the same pattern a third time, then a fourth time, and still he had no luck. At this point he had been in the water about thirty minutes and his air supply was becoming critical so he returned to his boat and used the portable pump he had brought with to refill the tanks.

Once back in the water he continued his search pattern. Suddenly he came upon a pickup, sitting serenely at the bottom of the lake. When he was renting his boat at the Boat Loft, the attendant was telling someone the story of how one of the cabin owners would drive his pickup across the lake in the winter so he could go ice fishing, and how one time he didn't come back. They were convinced he had fallen through the ice, pickup and all. He wondered if this was the pickup they were talking about. He swam over to it and peeked in through the window and sure enough, there was a man sitting in the driver's seat, still holding on to the steering wheel as if he was on his way to his cabin. Apparently, the fish couldn't get to him because all the windows were closed, so he was just privately decaying away.

The assassin surged slightly backwards, creeped out by the experience. He hated being in the water anyways, and this just reinforced his fears. Why did he have to be the one that would find this pickup?

He continued his search, back and forth and was again nearing the end of his oxygen supply when he saw something sparkling off in the distance. "Probably another beer can," he mumbled to himself as he swam towards the object. He was in luck. It was the drone. But now what? He really hadn't thought through what he was going to do if he found the drone, probably because he wasn't expecting to find it. Here it was and now what?

He had thought ahead enough to bring a short piece of rope with him. He tied one end to the drone and the other end to his diving belt. Then, because his air was starting to run low, he knew he needed to hustle to the surface. Since the drone was lighter under water, he was successfully able to drag it behind him toward the boat. When he arrived at the boat, he was nervous about someone watching him from one of the many cabins around the lake so he untied the end of the rope that was on his belt and tied it to one of the docking ties on the boat.

He climbed into the boat, removed his scuba gear, and started the boat, driving it slowly to a part of the lake where there were no cabins and where no one would see him. He started to pull on the rope, hoping to bring the drone on board the boat, when suddenly the drone slipped loose. He could feel the rope suddenly lose its pull and he realized what had happened so he quickly dove into the water hoping to retrieve the drone. That turned out to be the right move because he was able to recover the rope tied to the drone and pull it back to the water's surface. It was too heavy for him to lift on to the boat while he was swimming so he retied the drone to the end of the rope, again climbed aboard the boat, and then slowly, carefully, and successfully pulled the drone on board.

He had the drone. It was waterlogged and covered with river weeds, but he had it and he had the weapons system that was attached to it. Now he realized that he had another problem. How was he going to get the drone from the boat to the back of the pickup?

He spent some time pondering this next dilemma. Then he remembered a section of lake road that ran beyond the Boat Loft where he had rented the boat. He remembered how at certain points it ran close to the edge of the lake, but slightly up from the lake. If he waited till it was dark, he could deposit the drone somewhere along this stretch. He would return the boat and then drive the pickup to the location where he had left the drone, recovered the drone, and made his way out of the Holter Lake area.

He was feeling pretty proud of himself. He thought he had everything figured out and he was busy patting himself on the back, but his struggles had just begun.

He executed his plan. Recovered the drone, which was challenging because of its size and weight, loaded it into the pickup, returned the boat, and headed back to Helena. He went directly to the two-car storage shelter that he had rented for his previous assignment, and which was still in his name. Once there he removed the drone from the back of the pickup and departed from the storage shed. He returned to his hotel. Tomorrow the work would begin. He would work on cleaning up and reconstructing the drone and the drone's controller. He would test all of his equipment out, including the firing mechanism and the sights. He would test fire it and hopefully everything would function correctly. But there were a lot of "ifs" in this equation and just one of those if's could mean that the entire mission wasn't going to work. It would be a very anxious and stressful day.

SIXTEEN

After Jill left the conference room and refused to respond to Matthew's call for her to return, Matthew was irate. He barked at his FBI team in the conference room of the Helena police department, "We're letting the local police outthink us and outsmart us. This is entirely unacceptable. Why didn't we think of tracking the frequency of the drone? What's the matter with you guys? We're supposed to be smarter, better trained, agents." Then he turned to his techie in the room, Hilda Bittpicker and commanded, "Figure it out and report back to me what you've learned."

"Yes sir," was her response, even though she wasn't altogether sure how to figure out what the frequency was and if they even had the equipment available in the FBI to do the tracking. She decided that she had better buddy up to Samuel, from the local police force, and find out what he learned rather than trying to reinvent the wheel. She also knew that if she asked permission from Matthew to allow her to meet with Samuel, he would refuse to let her stoop that low. She was on her own and she had to come up with answers and fast.

Matthew wasn't done with his rant, "We have this list of thirty-two unidentified drones. What are we doing on tying those down?"

Another agent spoke up, "We've cleared eleven of them, nine are new. We just received them yesterday and we're working on them. That leaves twelve untouched. Of those twelve we have three that are causing a great deal of concern. The remaining nine are being put on some agent's list to go and identify, but the work has not yet been completed."

Matthew came back, "If I understand your numbers, we have twenty-one where we haven't done anything and that's just not acceptable. Get agents out on them immediately. Stress the importance and urgency of what they are doing. I want answers by tomorrow."

"Yes sir," replied the agent.

"Tell me more about the three that you say are causing a great deal of concern," questioned Matthew.

"We haven't been able to locate either the owner or the drone," responded the agent. "We haven't given up; we just don't know where those three drones are which puts them and their owners on the top of our suspect list. One of them has reported their drone as stolen, which makes it even more challenging."

"If Hilda figures out this frequency tracking thing, we should be able to locate the missing drones, assuming they are within the same vicinity where they were last located. Is that true Hilda?" challenged Matthew.

"Yes," responded Hilda. "That would actually be easier because we will know the frequency of those specific drones because we will know their serial numbers and they will be much easier to track as long as they are within range of the tracking equipment."

"Get her the frequencies and their original locations," commanded Matthew. "What else are we doing on this case?" Matthew asked the room.

"We're dissecting the videos of the drone," responded another agent, "and we found a couple more home videos which show the drone, but none of those are any clearer or give us any more information than the one we received is from the commander's neighbor. That's still our best one. The other videos give us the direction that the drone came from or returned to but that really doesn't tell us a lot."

"Does the airport control tower, or satellite help us in any way?" asked Matthew.

"Neither of them are looking for something as small as a drone," responded still another agent.

"We need to get into this killer's head," recommended the same agent. "Do we have access to a profiler?"

"Or maybe a Ouija board," mocked Matthew. After a pause he said, "Actually, that's probably not a bad idea. I'll have a profiler join our team."

"Any more ideas?" asked Matthew. After a pause and when no one spoke up he said, "Let's get to work and get this guy!"

With the meeting over, and everyone in the FBI team rummaging around with their team members, Hilda left the conference room. This wasn't unusual. They just assumed she was taking a potty break or getting coffee. However, she went directly to Samuel Ledger's desk, sat down beside him and in a casual, friendly voice asked, "I understand you've made an excellent breakthrough on tracking what might actually be the drone that we're searching for. Do you mind telling me about it?"

Samuel, being a techie who loved attention and to have that magnified by a girl's interest, said, "Of course. What do you want to know?"

Both Samuel and Hilda had previously noticed each other, since they stood out from the rest of the blue suit and tie crowd. Samuel was a short, five foot ten, a completely geeked out individual, with the hair on the sides of his head shaved off and wearing a "Big Bang Theory" t-shirt. He was convinced that he had every geek's dream job doing data searches for the police.

Hilda wasn't much better. She was a complete deviation away from the FBI's rules. She was the same height as Samuel Ledger, with geeked out bright green rimmed glasses and a blue streak through her long hair that had orange tips on the bottom ends of her hair. Several FBI team leaders had tried to get her fired, claiming she wasn't FBI material, but her genius abilities in research and computer analysis had caused key people to overlook her defiance. One manager had commented, "She's worth five of my other agents. She can look as weird as she wants. I just won't put her into the field, and she seems quite happy staying behind a desk with her computers."

There was an immediate attraction between Samuel and Hilda. It had very little to do with the job and everything to do with the geek bond they felt for each other.

Samuel was the first to make a move and asked, "I'll tell you whatever you want, but you have to agree to go out to dinner with me tonight."

"I thought you'd never ask," responded Hilda, and their relationship was off and running.

SEVENTEEN

He had the drone in his garage storage unit. He still had the tarp that he had used previously to cover the drone. The real problem was working on the drone and the controller, making sure they were in sync with each other and working properly.

He returned to his lighted two-car storage unit where he could drive the pickup in, shut the door and go to work. The three-month rental hadn't expired so it was still available for him to use. He decided that he still had the option of sleeping on the back seat of the pickup for a night or two if that's what it took. But he preferred the hotel for a solid night's sleep.

He checked messages on his smartphone and found an email from his employer which included a name and a picture. It read, "Kate Burkenstead, consultant and advisor to the military." He spread out his tools and started working on the drone and its controller.

He tried to start the drone but it wouldn't start. He assumed it was the battery. He opened the battery casing and found the battery completely discharged. He dried the battery off and tried charging it using the small generator that he carried in his pickup for exactly that reason. If the battery didn't charge, he would be stuck because it was a special-order unit and he wouldn't be able to get a replacement in any of the local stores.

The charge time was two hours so while it was charging, he worked on the remainder of the drone, checking the props and the engine and cleaning out debris that had accumulated in the short time it was in the water. He felt he had a reasonable chance of getting it working since none of the prop blades had been broken off.

Two hours went by quickly because he had been kept busy with the cleanup and repairs. He reinstalled the battery into the unit and tried to start it. It started, but then immediately sputtered to a stop. He tried again with the same result. It left him scratching his head, confused as to what could possibly be wrong. He checked the battery and it seemed to be connected correctly. And it seemed to be holding a charge. He checked the engine and it seemed clean. He concluded that for some reason the engine wasn't working properly. It seemed to jam up. He was getting frustrated so he decided to work on something else. He started checking out the weapons system to make sure it was operational. It was full of dirt and other crud. Since it was mounted under the drone, it had been buried in the dirt when the drone hit the bottom of the lake. Ironically, it also contained the most sensitive equipment, including the targeting system and the firing mechanism. If he couldn't get that working, then what use was there in getting the drone working?

He always carried some blanks precisely for testing purposes. He put some blanks into the six-shooter revolver that had been converted to a rifle for long range accuracy. He fired up the controller, checked the screen on the targeting system, and found that the picture wasn't coming through.

In frustration he threw up his arms and yelled, "This is a mess!"

He opened the garage door, climbed into his pickup, drove out of the storage shed, shut the door, locked it, and drove off to find a drink somewhere. He needed some head space. Maybe he would be able to figure this out with a clearer head.

EIGHTEEN

Matthew Christ stormed into Jill's office without knocking. He walked up to her desk and started talking, uncaring whether she was busy or not. "Why is your department not supporting the FBI's effort to find this serial killer?"

Jill, extremely irritated by his insinuation, looked up and said, "What? Everything you have received from us. At this point you and your team have accomplished nothing. I have no interest in your whining, not after my team spent days trying to track down the owners of these drones and then handing you the information. What have you accomplished with that information?"

"I don't answer to you," responded Matthew. "What we do stays within the confines of FBI and isn't open to your review and inspection. The reason I'm here is you have agents that are interfering with our investigation. They are tracking the drone and they are not willing to share that information with us. I'm thinking of pressing charges against your team for obstruction of justice."

"Go for it you idiot," barked Jill. "Then see what cooperation you get from us, realizing that everything you have so far is from us. So far you and your team have been worthless. We would be much further along in this process if it wasn't for the obstructions your team has caused to our investigation. But, as you say, it's your investigation, so have at it."

Just then the Chief of Police arrived, entered Jill's office, and asked, "What's going on between you two? You seemed to work well together before on the Falcon murders, but now everyone is commenting about the level of tension between you. What's the story?"

"She's obstructing our investigation," Matthew blurted out.

"How?" asked the Chief.

"Someone in her department is tracking the drone and she refuses to share that information with us," insisted Matthew.

"What's the story?" the Chief asked Jill.

"You know Samuel Ledger is a techie genius. At home and on his own time he designed a piece of equipment that searched for signals going back and forth between a drone and its controller in the frequency range of the drones that we are searching for. He was not on the payroll at the time and what he came up with is not something I can take from him and order him to turn it over to the FBI. It's his equipment and he shared it with us simply because he wants us to track down this killer. Unfortunately, so far, he really doesn't have anything concrete. He only has a partial transmission and there have not been any repeat transmissions. We're not even sure the small signal he received is anything of value. We're not sure he's tracking the right unit because it wasn't in the area of any of the murders. We're waiting for more signals to see if we have anything. I went into the FBI's conference room and already shared all this information with them. There is nothing else to share so I'm not sure where the obstruction accusation is coming from."

"We demand to know how he's getting this signal," barked Matthew.

"Have you asked Samuel?" responded Jill.

"I shouldn't have to. You should have already done that," was Matthew's comeback.

"Have Samuel come here," the Chief instructed Jill.

Jill picked up her phone's receiver, dialed a number, and said, "Samuel Ledger! Can you come into my office?"

The room went quiet while they waited. Soon Samuel entered the room and Matthew immediately went on the attack, "So you're the guy that's withholding information from my team!"

"What are you talking about?" asked Samuel.

"The tracking system! You're the one hiding it from our team. I ought to have you arrested for obstruction of justice!" Matthew continued his rant.

"Who is this butthead?" asked Samuel directing the question to Jill.

"He's the lead FBI detective working on the drone murder case," Jill responded.

"Then he's not very good at communicating with his team," answered Samuel, who was never known for his patience, especially when he was being attacked. "I want him arrested for false arrest and defamation of character. I spent most of the evening showing Hilda, who is the FBI techie on his team, my tracking tool on my own time. I'm doing this on my own with my own equipment and I owe nothing to this idiot. I explained to Hilda how it works and what I've seen. She has all the information and has seen it in operation. She says that she doubts the FBI has comparable equipment. I was thinking of letting her use my personal equipment but now that I've been harassed by this arrogant idiot there's no chance that you're going to get access to my personal stuff. That would be entirely stupid. And if he attacks me like that again, I'll file a formal complaint. I demand this jerk apologize immediately or my next act will be to file that complaint!"

Matthew's answer only added fuel to the fire, "You have no right to keep anything from us!"

"Talk to your team you stupid idiot," barked Samuel, "and don't ever come around me again. I already gave them all the information and apparently you don't communicate very successfully with your team members, or you'd know that. There is nothing else for me to give to you that I haven't already given. I even gave her the frequency of the drone that I was tracking and she's going to use that to try and tie down the killer drone. However, we don't know for sure that my drone is the killer drone so we can't really stop working on all the remaining drones. But it's a lead that she's going to follow up anyway."

Matthew stormed out of the room without saying another word and Samuel asked the Chief, "How do I file a formal complaint against an FBI agent?"

"I'd rather you didn't," responded the chief, "but I can see that you're going to pursue this regardless so I'll show you the procedure."

"There is irony here," Samuel explained. "Hilda was going to make a formal request to him to have me transferred to the FBI team. There's very little chance of that happening, especially after I file this complaint."

The chief chuckled. Then Jill spoke up and added, "Then I should file a complaint as well."

"About what?" asked the Chief.

"All this tension with Matthew was caused when I refused his advances," she explained as she started to choke up and tears welled up in her eyes. "The FBI should know that he tried to sexually intimidate me and since I refused him, he has been hostile to me which makes it impossible to work with him."

"That's upsetting to me," responded the Chief. "My wife was also sexually harassed at work and in spite of my repeatedly telling her to file a complaint, she never did. She had to work in an environment of intimidation for five years. Now that you've told me about this intimidation by Matthew, I strongly recommend that both of you file your individual complaints and you have my complete support."

"Sorry for the tears," added Jill. "I just found out I'm pregnant which is making me hormonal."

"Congratulations," both the chief and Samuel burst out saying. Their angry faces suddenly transformed into smiles.

"That's the best news I've had all day," added the Chief.

"Thanks," responded Jill.

Then the Chief went around her desk and said, "Let me use your computer for a second and I'll show you how to file that complaint."

Jill went to work on the complaint and the chief told Samuel, "Show me your computer and I'll help you get started on your complaint as well."

"Excellent," said Samuel as the two of them left Jill's office.

Two hours later Matthew came storming into Jill's office, shut the door behind him, and started cussing. "Why does internal affairs want to talk to me? Is this something you and the weirdo employee of yours have cooked up? I'm trying to solve a serial murder case and I don't need to waste my time with some internal affairs investigation."

Jill, tired of Matthew's rants, simply said, "Get out of my office and leave me alone before I have reason to file another report about your behavior."

Matthew, frustrated that Jill wasn't responding how he had hoped, stormed out of her office and slammed the door behind him.

Jill proceeded to place an addendum to her complaint discussing how his continued behavior was unacceptable.

NINETEEN

Kate continued her interviews and her search through the base communications records. She knew that anyone smart enough to pull something like this off should know better than to use common communications methods that everyone uses. On the other hand, if they weren't that smart and she hadn't done this search she would feel really stupid.

As expected, her interviews revealed nothing out of the ordinary and the communications search wasn't doing much better. She had laid her trap and she had narrowed down the search, but that also meant that she wouldn't be able to use that tool again. Being connected with the military meant that she wasn't restricted by civilian rules, so her next trick would be to place tracking devices on each of the leadership's vehicles and then to use tracking software to see where they ventured. She would look for common meeting places between multiple individuals or regular visits to specific locations which could be drop-off points for messages.

She planned to continue the interviews and message searches while the tracking software recorded their movements. The software noted the location of each of their homes, and their places of work, and didn't highlight them as possible drop-off points. But it would raise flags on regularly visited places or out-of-the way movements that didn't fit shopping, home or work. Her next step would be to place remote cameras in these locations and watch what happened. Her hope was to narrow down the twenty potential suspects and end up with only two or three. Better yet, maybe only one would come to the surface.

She was quick to place the tracking devices on her first batch of the vehicles. She couldn't do all of them at once since the software didn't allow it. In three of the cases, she had to track multiple vehicles for the same individual, because they would switch between vehicles, but the software would handle GPS tracking for up to twenty vehicles, so she wasn't worried. She felt confident that she would soon have the evil monster in-hand.

With the trackers and the software in place she was able to relax for another weekend. Besides, it would often take a few weeks of tracking before the repeated stops could be detected.

It was Friday night and Kate had country dancing on the brain. Dick had invited her to a western bar in Butte where his band was playing. It was about a one-hour drive south on Interstate 15. She was tired of talking and tracking and she was ready for a relaxing evening. She left the base around five, grabbed her Taco Treat Enchatreato for dinner, and went to her hotel. She changed into something more appropriate for a dance bar, hopped into her car and headed south.

Her car's GPS directed her perfectly to the bar/restaurant that she was searching for. At the door they asked for an entrance fee but when she explained that she was an invited guest of the band they let her enter without paying the fee.

It was about a half hour before the start of the music. She was directed to the band table and she made her way there. The band was just finishing up their warm-ups when she arrived and they all greeted her and acted happy to see her, especially Dick. She was excited because this had the making of another fun evening.

About five minutes before the band started playing, she received a beep on her phone which indicated an important message. Checking her phone, she saw a Facebook message from her boss that read, "The rumor mill has it that there may be a contract out on you. Be careful!"

Suddenly her entire attitude changed from one of being excited to one of being concerned. Who would put a contract out on her? And why? Then she thought about the murder of Commander Mark Simeon and she had to wonder if that was a contract as well. And possibly executed by the same people? Was she slated to be the next victim of the Drone Killer?

Dick could see that Kate was suddenly preoccupied so he asked, "Is something wrong? I noticed that you read a message and now you seem disturbed. Is there something I can do to help?"

"Keep me distracted," was her response. "It's about work, and I don't want that to weigh me down tonight."

"I'll do my best," responded Dick. "But first I have to play some music." He stood up with the rest of his band members and they each went directly toward their instruments.

It was much easier to say she wanted to be distracted than it was to actually be distracted. Should she drop out of the mole hunt project that she was working on? Her mind kept racing through everything, wondering if the contract placed on her was actually about one of her previous assignments or about her current assignment. She just wasn't sure what the connection was and that worried her. Maybe if she knew more, she could be more careful.

In spite of being distracted, she still had a fun, somewhat relaxing, evening. She enjoyed the company of the band members and of course Dick. At the end of the evening of dancing and socializing Dick asked her, "Are we going to see you tomorrow at our other gig in Helena?"

"Of course," she responded. "I wouldn't miss it."

"Maybe you won't be as distracted by work," he suggested.

"I'm sorry if I seemed distracted," she said, "but I had a really fun evening anyways. Thanks a lot."

She felt bad for being distracted, but if Dick knew the reason behind it, she was convinced he would understand. But that message wasn't the type of message you would share with someone you had recently met. It would potentially scare them off.

The drive home to the hotel took about an hour and then she slipped into the hotel room, always looking around and over her shoulders to see if there was a drone or an assassin lurking around the next corner.

The next day, Saturday, was spent thinking and reviewing. Around midday she received a surprise call from Dick, "Can I take you to lunch?"

Still being cautious, Jill responded, "I could meet you somewhere. Where would you like to go?"

"You're probably working. I was worried about you this morning. You seemed to be really bothered by that message and I just wanted to get you away from work for an hour or so. Are you up to it?"

"Sure. Where do you want to go?" Kate responded.

"I'll meet you at the Taco Treat," said Dick. "You mentioned you like that place and I've never been there so I'd like to try it. Can we meet there in about thirty minutes?"

"Love it," said an excited Kate. "See you then."

Exactly thirty minutes later the two met in the Taco Treat restaurant where she introduced him to the beef Enchatreato. "You're going to love this," was her only comment. And she was thrilled when he did.

"Now, you have to tell me what's been on your mind," Dick asked. "What's been bothering you?"

"It's just work," she replied, attempting to soft shoe what was really happening. "It can get stressful at times, especially since my job is solving problems that often are connected with corruption. And people don't like to be exposed. Often there are threats involved."

"Who are you working for?" asked Dick.

"The Army National Guard," she responded.

"So, what are you working on?" he asked.

"Sorry but I really can't tell you any more," she answered. "It's not that I don't trust you, it's just that I am under oath and am legally not allowed to share what I'm doing with anyone, included most of the people in the Army National Guard."

"Well, I can see how that can get stressful," he said. "If there is anything I can do to help, I hope you'll tell me."

"I appreciate the offer but you really can't get involved."

Dick said, "Are you busy this afternoon? I'm heading over to the rodeo grounds because they're having an exhibition of Argentinean and Mongolian cowboys and I've heard it's supposed to be impressive."

Kate thought for a moment about how she should concentrate on the work she was doing, and then she remembered the message about there being a contract on her and she decided, the heck with it, I'm gonna have some fun. Let's see if the drone killer can find me at a rodeo.

She responded, "Let's do it. It sounds fun."

Dick said, "let's hop into my car and I'll take you to the fairgrounds. That's where the rodeo grounds are located and where the exhibition is going to be held. We can stay there for a little longer and watch the rodeo too, but then I have to leave because I have to play with the band tonight."

"I'll have to drive separately so I can return to the hotel afterwards and get changed," responded Kate. "I'll drive to your gig separately and join you."

"Perfect," responded Dick. The two went out to their cars and jumped in. Soon they were off to the State Fairgrounds. It didn't take long and soon after arriving they found a parking spot. There was quite a large crowd heading for the rodeo grounds. The planned exhibition had quite a large following.

After finding a spot on the bleachers, Kate and Dick prepared for the upcoming event by studying the program for the evening. It included the exhibition by the two international groups and then the following rodeo events. It looked like a fun and long evening.

At three in the afternoon, as per the schedule, the announcer had everyone stand for the national anthem, and then announced the first part of the program by saying, "The first event of the evening will be a demonstration of Argentinean cowboy skills. These will be demonstrated by the gauchos from Buenos Aires. They use boleadoras, which are three hard rock leather balls tied to a rope and they use this much like we use a lasso to capture cattle that are trying to escape. We hope you enjoy their demonstration,"

With that a group of five gauchos entered the ring and made quick work of the cattle that were scrambling around attempting to avoid capture. The Montana audience was more than impressed by the gaucho skills and applauded and cheered their activities. The demonstration went on for about thirty minutes.

Next on the agenda, the announcer said, "Now we have a demonstration of the cowboy skills coming from Mongolia. These cowboys come from Ulaanbaatar. You'll notice that they use long sticks looped with rope on the end and work from the ground rather than from horseback to capture their prey. They also use much smaller horses. Note their clothing, especially their boots. They are quite colorful and impressive with two and sometimes more layers. So let the show begin."

A group of about five Mongolian cowboys entered the ring followed by a large herd of their smaller horses. The cowboys went to work immediately, capturing their prey with their long sticks. Once again, the Montana audience was thoroughly impressed and excited to watch these cowboys at work. Their show also lasted about thirty minutes.

Kate was completely fascinated and impressed by these two groups of cowboys. "It's amazing how each of them independently developed the skills necessary to accomplish their ranching goals," commented Kate to Dick.

"I think it's pretty amazing as well," he responded. "That's why I was anxious to come and watch this demonstration."

"Thanks for bringing me," said Kate.

Then the announcer rehearsed the remainder of the program, announcing the rodeo competition was about to begin. He said,

"We'll go ahead with the main part of the competition, starting with the bull riding competition." Then he announced the first rider.

Kate and Dick continued to watch through the first few events, and then Dick said, "Sorry but I need to get going."

"Of course," responded Kate and the two of them got up to leave.

The fun was over and Kate said, "I'll go back to the hotel. I'll be there at your gig tonight for sure," she warned Dick.

They walked to the parking lot and parted, each going their separate way. The rest of the afternoon, which wasn't much more than an hour, was spent going through the tracking traces that had been recorded over the last days. It had only been a few days since she started the tracking and it usually took at least a couple weeks before there were any meaningful results. There wouldn't be anything repetitious this early. In spite of realizing that it was still early for results, she found it interesting to look for patterns. One pattern that jumped out at her almost immediately was that two individuals seemed to meet up at the same place twice over the last few days. The location turned out to be a hotel, which suggested an affair or some clandestine meeting. When she checked into who those individuals where she was surprised to discover that it was Commander Planter and VC Forengi. Obviously these two knew each other better than they had let on in the past. Kate immediately realized that Forengi's friendly attitude was all about weeding information from her for the Commander. She decided that she would place a remote camera at the hotel and hopefully she would learn if they were just sharing information, or if there was something more sexual to these meetings. She strongly suspected the latter.

Evening didn't come quick enough for Kate. She wasn't going to let that message about a contract on her, or the potential betrayal by VC Forengi ruin another evening, but she remained cautious and was on the constant lookout for a drone in the sky.

TWENTY

FLASHBACK (thirty years - when Brack Heldinger grew up as a Navy brat) - When he was ten years old his father was stationed at the Whidbey Island Naval Air Station and worked as a mechanic. His father was a brutal and unforgiving man and life at home in Navy housing on the peninsula south of Oak Harbor, the islands biggest city, was often traumatic.

Brack was stronger than normal for his age and he loved his mother but hated how his father treated her. Brack was also bullied at home, and he transferred that behavior to the kids at school. He became the school's bully. He was slightly overweight, which came as a result of his mother's poor eating habits, constantly thriving on fast food and unhealthy snacks. She was seriously overweight at about three hundred pounds.

His mom seemed to constantly have bruises on her face and arms from the beatings that his father would regularly give her. Brack resented his father's tendency toward violence and was occasionally given hard slaps across the face as well. The house was a mess because it was so painful for his mother to move around. Everything seemed to hurt including her back, her legs, and her arms. Additionally, she was a bit of a hoarder, hitting every garbage bin and garage sale and collecting all the "treasures" that she said she "couldn't believe people would actually throw away." The home was still livable, but occasionally it became a struggle to get from one room to the next.

His father drank most of his meals, and between the drinking and the gambling, the family barely scraped by trying to get enough food for the table. His father was five foot ten and gruff looking. His eyes seemed to always get glazed over from his bad lifestyle habits. His hair was rarely neat. And he had a scar on his left cheek from a fight he had gotten into several years earlier.

One evening around ten PM, when Brack and his mom were home alone, his father came storming into the house drunk and demanding, "Where's dinner? I expect dinner to be ready and waiting for me when I come home. Why are you just sitting around watching television when I'm here starving?"

"We had dinner ready for you at seven but you didn't show up so I put everything away," responded the mom.

"It doesn't matter when I come home," he barked. "You're supposed to be ready for me whenever. Otherwise, what purpose do you serve? I do all the hard work around here and all you have to do is take care of me and that brat of yours. Get your fat ass off the couch and get me my dinner!"

"Seriously?" responded the mom. "You come in here drunker than a skunk and talk about me slacking off! You have some nerve."

The father flew into a rage, stumbled over to the couch, grabbed the mother by the hair and yanked her up off the couch. His mother screamed, "What are you doing you savage? That hurts. Leave me alone!"

The mom was hunkered over because of the way he was pulling her off the couch. She knew how to get her revenge and she punched her husband several times as hard as she could in the balls. The husband screamed in pain, let go of her hair, and collapsed to the floor. The mom, struggling to get up because of her weight, started to walk around him and he gave her a swift kick in one of her legs, knocking the leg out from under her. She tripped and started to fall, crashing her head into the glass coffee table as she came to the ground.

Brack knew what he wanted to do. He had been planning for this day, and he knew how he was going to respond. He ran to his parents' bedroom and grabbed a pistol out of the nightstand drawer. He cocked the pistol and returned to where his father was laying on the ground, still rubbing and comforting his balls. Brack didn't hesitate. He saw his mother knocked down and he wasn't sure if she was alive or dead, but he knew what he was going to do next before he also became a victim of his father's brutality. He aimed the pistol at his father's head and fired, shooting him close to his left ear. The first shot didn't seem to do the job because his father looked up at him with an expression on his face which said, "What the heck do you think you're doing?"

Brack fired a second time, this time it hit his father's left eye. There was no longer any movement from the father. Brack knew he was dead. Then he rushed over to his mother to see if she was alive. Sadly, he discovered she was also dead, having received a gash in her forehead which still had a glass shard sticking partially out of it.

Brack had to think fast. He knew the neighbors probably heard the gunshots and would have called the police. He took the gun, wiped it down for fingerprints, put it into his mother's hands, making sure her fingerprints were all over the gun, and then dropped the gun next to her body. She would no longer be able to contradict what had happened so she might as well take the blame for the shooting. It would be her ironic revenge.

Having staged the murder, the way he wanted it to look, he ran out the front door screaming, "My parents are dead. They just killed each other!"

The neighbors all came running out to see what all the commotion was about and a few minutes later the police arrived at the scene. Brack told them his version of what had happened claiming, "I didn't see it happen because I was in my bedroom, but my dad was yelling at my mom about dinner then I heard a crash and shots being fired, all about the same time. I rushed out of my room to see that they were both laying there dead just like they still are. I didn't know what to do."

He claimed innocence and the police had no reason not to believe him so they recorded his statement. Then the officer in charge said, Child Protective Services (CPS) will be here shortly and they will bring you somewhere safe. Just wait here till they arrive."

Brack immediately translated that to mean that he was going to be placed into some kind of foster care system and he didn't want anything to do with that. He waited until he was sure no one was watching, and then he slowly walked away from the scene. Whidbey Island was beautifully covered with forest land and there were lots of places to hide. Unfortunately, it also rained a lot so Brack knew he would need to find shelter. He stayed on the base, hiding out close to his home, and in the middle of the night he snuck back into the house, bundled up some warmer clothes and a coat, took one of the hidden pistols that his father had kept around for protection, grabbed a tent and sleeping bag out of the garage, and returned to his forest hideaway.

His father was his first murder, but it wouldn't be his last. He travelled to Seattle where he connected with the seedy side of town and got connected with one of the gangs. It wasn't long before he was actively involved with selling drugs, even though he never indulged in them himself. He became practiced in weapons and became an expert marksman.

Brack's next jump in his growth as an assassin occurred about eight years later when one day a gang member friend asked him if he knew anyone who could execute a contract. Brack asked, "What is it he wants done?"

"He wants to get rid of his wife," was the response.

Brack responded with, "I can handle that. How much is he willing to pay?"

"He wasn't sure what the going price was for getting rid of a wife," answered the friend. "He wants her not just to get killed, but for her body to disappear as well. He wants nothing that will be traceable back to him."

"Naturally," responded Brack. "Tell him ten thousand for the execution and another ten thousand to get rid of the body. Half now and half after the job is complete." He had no idea what an execution would cost, but these numbers sounded good to him. Later his price would go up significantly.

"I'll let him know," responded the friend.

It was only about one hour later when Brack received a text from his friend which said, "You have the job. I'll bring you the details and the initial payment after I receive them."

Brack texted back, "Include pictures."

"Will do," was the response.

After receiving the details about the wife, he was also informed about a trip she would soon be taking. It turned out that the wife had family out on Whidbey Island in Langley and that she was heading out there from Seattle in a couple days for a visit. She would be using the night ferry from Mukilteo to Clinton which Brack felt was perfect. He could get rid of her and dump her into Possession Sound and be done with the contract all in one swoop.

The wife was on the ferry as planned. She made the mistake of wanting to go to the restroom on the upper deck of the ferry. She loved the view up there. The city lights all around were beautiful at night. She went to the restroom and then walked out onto the observation deck, which was perfect for what Brack had planned. He snuck out on the far side of the observation deck and moved slowly toward her location. As usual, there was no one else around. The trip to the island was short and most people chose to just wait in their vehicles. That helped to make the job easy for him.

She started to turn away from the observation deck as if she was going to return to the inside of the ferry when Brack took action. He used his silenced pistol and fired three quick shots at his target, hitting her twice in the body close to the heart, and once in the head. She slumped down and hit the ground. Brack then rushed over to her, picked he up with one hand under head and his second hand between her legs. He quickly lifted her up over the railing and dumped her over the side of the ferry.

The waters were rough that day making her splash into the water practically unnoticeable. Brack had executed his second murder and he was proud of himself, having earned a quick twenty thousand dollars.

TWENTY-ONE

FLASHBACK (continued) - Brack was getting tired of being a gang banger. He saw little future in it and wanted more. He loved the idea of being an expert marksman and felt that with a little more training he could become someone that was in high demand as an assassin. He felt that the best place to receive further training would be in the military so he joined the US Army.

In the military, Brack's shooting talents were quickly recognized and he was given sniper training. He was assigned to Fort Carson in El Paso, Colorado, which had a reputation as an excellent training base. He quickly moved up and was deployed to Afghanistan in the role of a sniper. Once there he earned a reputation as being trigger happy, at times shooting even when the target wasn't confirmed. He was occasionally reprimanded but didn't seem to care. After his deployment, and when his term of service was coming to an end, he decided he had accomplished his goal of becoming an expert marksman and he left the service. That was when he decided to branch out on his own.

Near the end of his time in the Army, when he was just a few months short of exiting, he got married, not so much because he had found his eternal soul mate, but because he wanted access to cheap sex, and he thought that getting married would solve that problem for him. He soon found out that his wife also had expectations from him and she had no problem telling him he was inadequate in meeting her needs. Strangely, she thought that she could get him to pay more attention to her if she had an affair and so she went out on him, which of course he found out about because that was part of the plan. Unfortunately for her he didn't react the way she had anticipated.

Brack responded to the news of her betrayal by developing a keen hatred for women. He decided that they were a tool that was to be used, and not tolerated. His first act of revenge was late one night when he drove up to Colorado Springs. He had been to the city several times because of the excellent German restaurants, and he loved the German food, but this time he was going there for a different reason. He took off his ring and drove to a topless bar close to the airport. He knew it would be easy to find a girl that, for a price, would be willing to give him a one-night stand. It was also an area that had lots of hotels so he would be able to take his hooker into a room and abuse her to his heart's content.

Everything was going according to plan. He went to the stripper bar and spent the evening watching boobs bouncing around. It wasn't long before a hooker approached him and sat down next to him, making conversation. She was a little on the chunky side and he liked his girls "slim and trim," as he would describe it, so he sent her away. Soon two more girls came to him, one sitting on each side of him. He liked the one on his left better than the one on his right and he asked her if she would come to the hotel with him, to which she readily agreed.

He left the bar with the girl hanging on his arm and took her to his car. They drove to a nearby sleezy hotel with outside access, and he asked for a room that was somewhat hidden from the main traffic. He booked a room. Once in the room Brack ripped at the girl's clothing, grabbing at her tits like a savage beast. Soon the two were naked and tucked away humping and bumping on the bed like a pair of rabid dogs.

Once Brack was satisfied he ended the evening by pulling out a small twenty-two pistol, which he had tucked away in a lower pocket of his cargo pants, placing the pistol on the hooker's left breast, and shooting. His actions were so quick that the girl didn't even have enough time to scream. He had targeted her in such a way that her heart would stop immediately thereby avoiding a lot of blood being pumped out of her body. The twenty-two round also didn't penetrate all the way through her body, which minimized leaving anything behind for ballistics.

Brack shot her a second time, just to make sure, this time through the eye, but he was sure she was dead because no blood was oozing out of her chest wound. Uncaringly he rolled her up in a bed sheet and carried her out to his car, throwing her in the back seat. He had gotten what he wanted out of her. He had used her in the way he wanted. Now he was done with her.

The hotel room was clean. There was no blood left behind and no sign that a murder had been committed. The only indication that there had been any kind of foul play was the missing bed sheet, and the hotel wouldn't even register that as a complaint.

Next, he drove her south down Highway 21, taking a left at Bradley Road. Shortly off to the right was a new housing development and he pulled into there. He found a new construction site where some trenches had been dug for sewer pipes. The pipes had already been laid, which was an indication that the trenches were about to be filled in. He dumped the hooker's body into one of the trenches, dropping her beside the sewer pipe and stuffing her as far down as possible. Next, he threw some dirt on her by pushing in the side of the trench. Making it look like the trench had slightly caved in and thereby successfully hiding her body.

The deed was done. His record, counting the kills he had successfully completed in Afghanistan, and his father and the contract murder in Seattle, was now at twenty. He had satisfied his lust, taken revenge on his wife, and successfully executed another kill. He was feeling pretty proud of himself as he drove south toward his home on the Army base.

Unfortunately, he still wasn't satisfied. He still felt betrayed by his wife and a hatred for women stewed in him and became stronger and stronger. His wife became a sex tool that he used violently, just like his father had taught him. He cared very little about her feelings or her needs. He would come home, use and abuse her in whatever way his current urge drove him, and then leave, discarding her like the tool that he thought she was.

At this point he was already planning to leave the military service so one day he travelled up to Colorado Springs searching out one of the local gangs. It wasn't hard to make the connection. They were highly visible. He approached one of the gang members and asked, "Who's your leader?"

"Why?" was the response he received from the gang member who looked at him skeptically.

"I have a proposal for him that can make us both rich," responded Brack.

"What kind of proposal?" asked the gang banger.

"I'm a sharpshooter and an assassin and can take out targets without anyone knowing who hit them and where the shot came from," responded Brack. "I can give your organization a reputation as contract experts. Do you think your boss would be interested?"

"I'm the boss and yes I'm interested," responded the gang leader. "I have a rival gang leader who is causing me some serious headaches and I would like to see him disappear. What would it take for you to do a hit on him?"

"Twenty Ks," was Brack's response, "and I'm giving you a discount at that just to establish our relationship."

"You do this for me and I'll get you lots more jobs, but I want a fifty percent cut in the future," responded the gang leader.

"Thirty percent," responded Brack.

"Forty," came back the gang leader.

The two bumped knuckles as a sign of agreement. Then Brack said, "Who is this rival gang leader that you want taken out?"

"It will be tough. He's careful and he has several guards that are always floating around him. He's rarely out in the open," responded the gang leader. Then he gave Brack the information that he needed about the rival gang leader so he could identify him when the time came. At this point Brack decided to change his name. His assassin's name would Brack Hellringer.

The two arranged for a method of communication between them using throw-away phones, and Brack left, feeling successful he had now initiated his new career as an assassin. His plan was that after he had a few successful hits under his belt he would move up to Denver and work with a larger and more prominent gang there and continue growing his reputation. Eventually he hoped to work his way into the assassination network where the money was enormous.

During his drive home he was feeling empowered. He was on a high. He saw a stupid girl hitchhiking along the side of the road and he decided to give her a ride. He needed someone that he could use to release his surge of adrenaline.

The girl climbed into his car and he drove off with her, making small conversation by asking where she was headed and what she was doing, to which she answered with what he was sure were a bunch of lies. He hated women and as far as he was concerned, they couldn't be trusted. Since she was going to lie to him, he felt it was his right to take advantage of her whatever way he wanted.

They were heading south on Highway 115 toward the base when Brack suddenly punched the girl in the chin. At first, she was just surprised and started screaming so he hit her again, this time successfully knocking her out. He exited on Norad Road and drove up into the Cheyenne Mountain area. He took a side road which seemed secluded and deserted. As he arrived at his destination she was starting to stir, waking up from his punch so he hit her again. This time she wasn't completely knocked out but she pretended to be out because she didn't want to be punched again. She knew what was going to happen, that she was going to be raped, and she hoped that it would be over with quickly.

He pulled her pants and underpants off of her. Then he also pulled up her shirt. He got off on her boobs, and then proceeded to screw her. The girl thought the torture was over with and expected Brack to dump her on the side of the road because that's what had happened the last time she was raped. He did dump her, but before he dumped her, he placed a twenty-two-caliber bullet in her heart and one in her eyeball.

He drug her out of the car and pulled her behind some trees. He threw a bunch of branches and leaves over her, hiding her as best he could. He couldn't see any reason to dig a shallow grave for her because the animals would just dig her up anyway and make dinner out of her body, so he decided to make it easy for them and leave her on the surface of the forest.

Now that he had accomplished his twenty-first murder, he was ready to go home. He was still turned on and maybe he would take sexual advantage of his wife anyway. Why not? That's what she was there for. And that's exactly what he did.

TWENTY-TWO

FLASHBACK (continued) - after having sex with his wife, Brack sat on the side of his bed and thought, Why am I keeping her around? She's just costing me money. I'd be better off without her around.

Brack started to formulate a plan. He had two months left of his military service and he had already decided that he was going to get out anyway, so how was he going to get rid of her in the next two months?

He knew that if she died in the house, he would immediately become the prime suspect. The spouse is always the prime suspect. So, he needed to get rid of her in a way that would leave him out of the picture. He needed an airtight alibi. It would need to be an accident and he couldn't be around when it happened.

Then he had another idea. What if she ran away from home? What if she just disappeared? He could forge a note where said she was tired of living with an abusive husband and she wanted to escape. Don't try to find her because she will change her name and probably be leaving the country. That would be easy to do. Then he would just need to make her disappear, which was easy enough to do in the Colorado wilderness.

Brack liked this new plan. It was easier to execute than trying to create an accident. He would take her fishing, maybe up in the Beaver Creek area or better yet in the Brush Hollow Reservoir. He would take his small fishing boat with and they would go out on the lake. He would stay out on the water until it was dark. Then he would use his silenced twenty-two pistol to put two bullets into her, weigh her down with the boat's anchor, and roll her over the side of the boat, never to be seen again.

Brack executed his plan the following Saturday, arriving around three in the afternoon. He drove up to the reservoir and launched the boat. The two of them floated out to the middle of the lake and started fishing. To the amazement of both of them they actually started catching a few fish, which was unusual because they often felt like they were cursed when it came to fishing, rarely catching anything. After it grew dark, they continued fishing, but Brack's wife kept a close eye on him because normally he would have quit fishing after a couple of hours but this time, they had been out here for over five hours, which was unusual for him. She was also suspicious because he rarely wanted to spend more than three minutes with her, which was about how long the sex lasted. She had kept the filleting knife handy in case anything suspicious happened.

Then it happened. Brack reached down into the lower pocket of his cargo shorts. His wife knew that this was where he kept his pistol and she grabbed the knife, just in case he aimed the gun at her, which had become what she suspected would happen. The pistol came out and sure enough he pointed it at her to which she responded by pointing the knife at him. He did not hesitate and fired a first shot but because she moved it hit her arm rather than her heart. She took the knife and swung it at him, but he was also quick to move and the filleting knife, which was exceptionally sharp, ended up being planted into his upper leg. It was so sharp that it went completely through the outside of his right leg, missing the bone. Unfortunately, while she was stabbing him, he also let off another shot, this time hitting her in the head.

Brack was angry about being stabbed and in revenge he completely unloaded the pistol into his wife, shooting her several more times in the heart and in the head. Then he tied the anchor to her left foot and dumped her over the side of the boat. He watched as she slowly sank down to the bottom of the lake. He had no regrets other than the knife sticking through his leg. The only thing he could think about was; This makes it twenty-two.

He turned his attention to the knife that was stuck in his leg. It was not bleeding too badly, and he knew that if he pulled the knife out it might cause the bleeding to increase so he left the knife in his leg and decided to work with it. He returned to the shore, secured the boat onto the trailer, and rushed off to the base for medical attention. The drive turned out to be painful because the knife was stuck partially into the seat of the vehicle and every bump in the dirt road wigged the knife. He eventually gave up, pulled out the knife, took off his shirt, and tied it tightly around the puncture marks of the knife, hoping to minimize the blood loss. Then he started driving like a maniac toward the emergency room of the base hospital.

The wound was quickly cleaned and stitched. Brack explained it was caused by a stupid accident where he was cutting at a side of meat and when he was plunging the knife into the meat, it slipped and ended up in his leg. They seemed to believe him and he soon left the emergency area.

Brack cursed his wife as he drove home. Once home he forged the note telling the world that she was leaving him, put it into an envelope, drove out to the nearest mail drop, and mailed it to himself. Earlier he had made sure her fingerprints had been on the paper and the envelope by handing it to her, and he hoped that would reduce any suspicion that Brack had orchestrated the entire disappearance.

But Brack still had another job to do. He had to execute the rival gang-leader. He had not even checked out the place where the rival gang hung out, and he would have to stake out that location before he would be able to determine how he was going to commit the assassination. He decided that would be how he spent his Sunday.

The following morning, he was still in a lot of pain from the cuts on his leg and he popped three Excedrin hoping that would dull the pain. Then he headed out to Colorado Springs and to the location that was supposed to be where the rival gang spent the majority of their time. It was where they had established their base for the distribution of their drugs. It was a small dingey looking mini mart which was connected to a nearby gas station. Brack parked in an obscure spot across the street and watched. He had brought a picture of the leader on his phone, and he watched to see if that individual could be spotted.

Brack had been sitting there for about one hour and so far, had not seen the leader. Then, to his surprise, three gang members walked from the convenience store across the street and came directly for his car. He first thought was to drive off, but then he thought that might just raise suspicions and possibly even get him shot at, so he rolled down his driver's side window and waited.

"What are you doing?" barked the lead gang member.

"I'm with a real estate company and we're thinking of buying this location and remodeling it," responded Brack. "I was watching to see what kind of street activity you had here." Brack decided this line should be innocent enough to where the gang members would leave him alone.

"We're not for sale, cracker," responded the gang member. "Get your ugly face out of here before we redesign it for you."

Brack was irritated by this gang member's aggressiveness and in his mind, he decided; I just might have to do a bonus free-bee assassination. He memorized the face of this rude individual and decided to drive around a little to see the best spot from where he could execute his plan. A roof close by would be perfect. He found the perfect spot. An abandoned building down the street and across the street from the mini mart. It had a flat roof which would be perfect for his needs.

Brack drove home, took a nap because he anticipated that it would be a long night ahead of him, and returned to the area around nine in the evening. He parked his car several houses down the street and across the street from the building he was planning to use for his stake out. He conveniently found a ladder lying on the ground next to the building, which looked like it was being used for some construction work on the building. He leaned the ladder up against the building and climbed onto the roof. From there he took down his backpack, which contained his collapsed target hunting rifle. He assembled the rifle, along with its silencer and, using the edging around the roof as a place to prop up his rifle, he prepared himself to wait for the appearance of the gang leader that he needed to target.

He waited one hour, then two, then three. He was starting to feel like he had made a mistake thinking this would be the location where he expected the gang leader to appear. So far, he had not seen any sign of the leader, in spite of all the activity at the mini mart had. There was a stream of people, in and out of the store, but no gang leader. Brack assumed they were all just purchasing drugs, because very few of the people came out of the shop with shopping bags. Most of them came out with their hands in their pockets.

Another hour passed and all of a sudden, the gang leader appeared, driving in a souped-up Cadillac. He stepped out of the car and moved toward the door of the mart. Unfortunately, Brack was not ready. He had become tired of staring through the scope and had gotten a little too comfortable sitting there on the roof and playing a game on his phone. He quickly jumped into position and prepared himself to take the shot. Fortunately, the gang leader was in no hurry to enter the store and was having a conversation with someone outside of the mini mart.

Brack was now ready. He prepared his shot, took careful aim, hoping to hit the gang leader with only one shot right through the heart. The person the gang banger was talking with was blocking the shot. However, Brack knew his weapon and his ammunition and he knew that he could shoot right through both of them. That would be too bad for the person standing in front of the gang leader, but Brack could not miss this perfect shot. He fired.

Both target individuals suddenly dropped to the ground. Then a cry went out amongst the gang members, and a flood of gang members came rushing out of the store. There was an unfortunate car driving past at the time and the gang members assumed that the car had something to do with the shooting, and they started firing on the car, which suddenly accelerated and raced away.

One of the individuals that came rushing out of the store was the individual who had confronted Brack earlier that day, and Brack decided that he could spare one more bullet. That would give him three hits for that day. He was proud of himself. Brack Hellringer had hit the number twenty-five.

And that is how Brack's career began. Soon the Colorado Springs gang that he was associated with started to receive a reputation as the place to go if you needed someone taken out. The price quickly rose from twenty thousand dollars to one-hundred thousand dollars. But that did not seem to slow down the takers. Customers were regularly coming down from Denver, then from as far away as Chicago. Brack's reputation became legendary, and soon he was contacted by a much larger crime organization, based out of Los Angeles. They made arrangements for Brack to join their team as the quintessential hit man for their organization, especially in highly visible political and business situations where the hits needed to be completely untraceable. Brack Hellinger, now named Brack Hellringer, was constantly in demand.

In all this time Brack's dislike for girls never changed. He always saw them as tools to be used and discarded. However, he eventually realized that he did not have to kill them after he used them. There were plenty of readily accessible girls in bars and pick-up joints who had minimal self-respect to the point where for a few drinks and a couple hundred bucks would buy them for the night, use them all he wanted to, and then send them on their way, never to see them again. He would often go to neighboring towns in order to make sure he never saw them again. That routine was easier and more convenient. He did not have to marry them. He did not have to live with them. And he did not have to put up with them.

At one point he did encounter one of his one-night stands and discovered that she had a small child walking with her. He quickly ditched from sight, hoping that she did not see him. Then he went to the county records department to check on the birth and discovered that the birth certificate did not have the name of a father associated with the child. He calculated backwards from the birth and realized that there was the possibility that he in fact might have been the father. Suddenly he became concerned about the fact that he might actually be a father, and that this child deserved to know who his father was. But what kind of father was he? Brack the assassin? Was that a father that the child should know? And being connected to a child would just give him a level of responsibility that he was not ready for. He decided that no way could he ever be a father.

Strangely Brack became concerned. How could he make a difference in this child's life without disrupting it? He made the decision that he would send the mother one million dollars along with a note that he suspected he was the father but he could not be a participative father but that he could at the very least help her with the upbringing of the child. It was chump change to him. He earned more than that on one assassination. He sent the money. At least it made him feel better about himself, at least for a few days. Now he could pat himself on the back and convince himself that he was some kind of good guy.

The mother of the child lived a very dejected life, having been outcast by her family because of her lifestyle. She was actively involved with numerous men, and that was how she made money. She had dropped out of high school and was only able to do the occasional fast-food job. Then, when she was pregnant, she could not even do that.

Since her parents had rejected her, and she didn't want to go back to them begging, her brother had stepped in and housed her through her pregnancy but after she had given birth, she decided that she didn't need her brother anymore and she didn't like his wife so she went to a shelter for new mothers and stayed there for a while. Since the shelter offered free childcare, she took advantage of that and returned to the only thing that she knew how to do well, prostitution. After about a year she had earned enough to where she was able to get her own small one-bedroom apartment, where she lived for the next few years. Often, she would lay her child down at night and once asleep she would sneak out, do a gig or two, and return a couple of hours later a couple hundred dollars richer. That was her life when she suddenly and unexpectedly received a money order in the mail for one million dollars. Initially she assumed it was a scam and she was about to rip up the check, but then she noticed and read the note.

"What the heck?" she barked. "Maybe this is real after all."

She went out and tried to cash the money order, and after a large amount of fuss, because no one believed she had really received a million dollars, she was eventually able to cash the money order by putting the money into a bank account. She was given an ATM card that she could use to withdraw up to three hundred dollars a day. She felt restricted, but also felt that three hundred a day extra cash would do nicely. Now she did not have to go out at night to do tricks with weird, gross, and obscene men.

She got a larger apartment in a nicer neighborhood, found herself a respectable job doing day care which also allowed her to bring her own child along. She was not going to be stupid, like a lot of Lottery winners blew their whole wad in a year. She was going to use this money to change her life and make herself respectable.

Eventually, after a couple of years of living a more complete life, she recontacted her parents and her brother, told them about her life, and invited them to come and see how she was living. They came, and with tears in their eyes were reunited.

Maybe Brack Hellringer actually did do something respectable in his cruel and abusive life after all.

TWENTY-THREE

IN THE PRESENT - Brack Hellringer was frustrated. He had retrieved the drone and its controller, but was all of that turning out to be a complete waste of time? Nothing seemed to work. He knew his next target was someone named Kate Burkenstead who was a consultant and advisor to the local military. And he wanted to use the same method for his attack on her, but in order to do that he needed to get his equipment working.

Brack could not get the drone started, and he assumed it was the battery, but if the battery was bad, it would be nearly impossible to mail order a replacement in time. Other than that, after he had cleaned up the unit, the drone seemed to be in working order. He had charged the battery, reinstalled it, and attempted to start the drone. It started, but then immediately sputtered to a stop. He tried several times with the same result. In frustration he had switched to working on the weapons system to make sure it was operational. He put some blanks into the six-shooter revolver that had been converted to a rifle for long range accuracy. He had fired up the remote controller and viewed the screen on the targeting system and found that the picture was not coming through. Nothing was working. The drone would not work. The targeting system was not operational, and the remote controller had a broken switch. How was he going to kill Kate?

Brack had left the garage for a few hours in order to get a bite to eat. When he returned, he tried to start the drone again and, to his surprise, it started up and worked. "It must have been water-logged and now it's dried out a little better," grumbled Brack under his breath, not really knowing what else could have suddenly caused it to work.

He went to the controller and hoped he would have the same kind of luck with that. However, it had not been under water, so it didn't need drying out. While he was out, he had purchased a small drill and some wood screws of various sizes. He drilled a small hole into the top of the controller where the knob had been broken off, and then inserted a thin screw into that location, not tightening it down too much so that it did not break the plastic of the controller. That seemed to work. Next, he tried firing up the controller to see if it would drive the drone and the targeting system. He slowly lifted the drone off the ground. Everything seemed to function properly with the drone's flight controls. Then he turned on the targeting system and found the screen still a little fuzzy. Regardless of its fuzziness, he fired a blank and found that the shooting mechanism worked. "I'll just have to go with it," grumbled Brack. He was frustrated that the targeting system was not clear, but he felt that it was clear enough for him to take a shot. The fuzzy image meant that he was not one hundred percent sure about the exact target, but it would be close enough for a kill shot.

Next, he would have to find out where Kate was located. He quickly learned that there were no Burkensteads as permanent residents in the Helena area, so he assumed she must be a visitor. He started calling the different hotels in the area, asking to be connected to Kate, and he kept hearing, "There is no Kate Burkenstead in this hotel." For some unknown reason, his own hotel was the last hotel he tried. And there she was. He had found her. His next job would be to stake out the hotel lobby and wait to see who she was. Then he would follow her and learn a little about her daily routine. Using this information, he would be able to figure out the best time and opportunity to take her out.

Following his plan, he sat in the lobby of the hotel and watched for her to leave. He had a picture of her that he had received with his contract information so he was able to recognize her when she came down the stairs and walked through the lobby. He jumped into action, got into his car, and started to follow her. He noted what car she was driving, and its license plate and in the future, he would watch the car rather than her. It would be too conspicuous if he were sitting in the lobby each day, and then would jump up when she walked through.

He followed her through the Starbucks drive-through off of the west end of Prospect Avenue. Then he followed her down Euclid Avenue to Custer Avenue where she turned west. After a few more turns they ended up at the Fort Harrison Montana Army National Guard Armory. That was where he had to drop off. He knew her route, and he had spotted several locations along the way where he would be able to perform his planned assassination, but the easiest would still be back at the hotel, bright and early in the morning.

Brack returned to his storage facility, hoping that his drone would perform better this time around. He tested the drone and its controller, but the performance wasn't any better than on the previous day. The drone seemed to work but the controller view screen for the firing mechanism was still fuzzy. He thought it was adequate for what he had to do so he planned on performing his execution of Kate in the morning, as she was heading out from the hotel for her car.

Early the following morning Brack was up and heading to his storage unit. He loaded the drone into the back of his pickup then drove back to the hotel. He checked to make sure that Kate's car was still in the parking lot. He drove around the back side of the hotel, making sure he was not being viewed by any of the security cameras. That became impossible. There were no blind spots. He drove to a nearby restaurant which had no cameras. He uncovered the drone and powered it up, slowly lifting it up off the back of the pickup. He flew the drone over to the hotel and set it down on the peak of the roof as a temporary holding place.

He returned into the hotel and went to a hallway window on the second floor from which it would be easy to watch Kate when she went to her car. It was about a thirty-minute wait before she exited the hotel and started her walk toward her car.

Brack raised the drone off the roof of the hotel and flew to the north side of the parking lot from which he hoped to get a better shooting angle. By now Kate was about two-thirds of the way to her car. Brack felt he had the perfect angle, but he lost a little confidence in his shot angle when the viewing screen was so unclear. He took aim and fired a shot. Unfortunately, rather than being a direct hit, the shot only grazed her.

Looking out of the hotel window, Brack could see that his shot was not a direct hit, so he fired two more shots. Kate fell to the ground and Brack assumed she had been killed.

That was when everything fell apart. The drone suddenly seemed to have a mind of its own. He was not sure if it was the battery that had lost power, or if some mechanism within the drone had given out. He would never have the opportunity to investigate. The drone suddenly darted into a tree and then crashed to the ground. Several people suddenly surrounded both Kate and the drone. It seemed like there were several individuals making calls to 9-1-1. But Brack knew he had to get away from the window and he desperately needed to dispose of the controller. The police would surely be searching the hotel. He was fortunate that there was a maid's cleaning cart in the hall. Its attendant was in one of the rooms and would not see him. At the end of the cart was a garbage bag and Brack quickly deposited the controller into the garbage bag and continued walking down the hall until he arrived at his room. He entered the room, shut the door, and leaned back against the door, relieved that he had not been spotted. This was a close call, one of the closest in his entire career. His equipment had failed miserably and would now be under the control of the police. However, all he could think of was; fifty-eight.

TWENTY-FOUR

Jill woke up in the morning feeling like throwing up. She ran to the bathroom and sure enough she successfully made a mess of the toilet. Eric rushed in behind her, placing his hand on her back, and asked the stupid question, "Are you okay?"

"Heck no I'm not okay," barked Jill. "I am puking into the toilet. How do you figure I am okay?"

Eric tried to keep his cool and asked, "Can I get you anything?"

"Crackers and pickles, and maybe a glass of milk," barked Jill. "And hurry it up."

Erick had heard about cravings when women were pregnant, but this combination of foods was just weird. But he was in no position to question her choices. He went off to the kitchen, pulled together what she selected, and rushed back to the bedroom.

When he arrived, she had returned to her bed. He put her food choices on the nightstand. She had closed her eyes and was turned away from him so he put his hand on her shoulder and sarcastically said, "I have breakfast for you."

She threw the blankets off and said, "I'm hot!"

"I know you are," was Eric 's response. It was a response he gave every time she said she was hot, but he played it with a different meaning and she knew what he meant, but she was not in the mood.

"Don't be an idiot," was her response. Then she sat up in bed and the first thing she ate was the pickle.

Jill and Eric normally had a very respectful relationship. Eric knew that Jill's negativity and frustration was because she was well into her pregnancy, so he felt he had to give her some slack since he knew he was the cause of the pregnancy. Despite Jill's short temper they both wanted this baby badly.

"I'm going to call in and tell them you're sick," suggested Eric.

"Just tell them I'm going to be a little late because I'm a little under the weather," responded Jill. Then she thought about it and said, "Actually tell them I will not be there until this afternoon. I understand Matthew is dealing with FBI internal affairs today and I would rather not be around for that brew-ha-ha anyway. But I need to go in this afternoon to meet Matthew's replacement."

"Hopefully he's not the intimidating idiot that Matthew was," responded Eric. "I can understand someone thinking I have a hot wife, because I do, but that doesn't give him the right to be disrespectful to you."

Jill's response was to rush off once again to the toilet.

For all the things we have heard about the ineptness of the FBI, there's one department that's efficient in the FBI and it is internal affairs. They were out visiting the Helena Montana office the very next day. Matthew was pulled into one of the interview rooms and two internal affairs officers jumped on him immediately, "Tell us about the conflict you're having with the Helena homicide detectives."

"They're refusing to share information with us," responded Matthew. "They're being their normal uncooperative selves."

"My understanding is that everything that you have on this investigation is from them," continued the investigator. "What have you developed on your own?"

"We finished all the searches for drones," responded Matthew.

"But that is after they narrowed it down to like three dozen, correct? And the ones that were left required visits to the homes which the local police here could not do or they would have had them done as well. Isn't that correct?"

Matthew was silent.

"Now the locals have figured out a way to track the drone, and all you have done is try to force them turn over what they have, even though it's not the property of the police. They have even given you the frequency of the drone that they suspect is the weapon. This leads to a drone out of Colorado that is apparently stolen. How much more can they do for you without solving the case for you? And now you are expecting a private citizen to turn his equipment over to you, just because he figured out something that all the brains in the FBI couldn't figure out? Is that correct?"

"He's a member of the police department and the local police are required to turn everything over to us," claimed Matthew.

"But this was something he did on his own, with his own equipment, and on his own time and therefore is not the property of the local police department. Isn't that correct?"

"That shouldn't make a difference," claimed Matthew.

"It makes a big difference and falls into the category of police harassment. And my understanding is that if you would have worked with him instead of making Gestapo type demands, he might have given the whole thing to you on a silver platter."

Again, Matthew was silent.

Next the interrogator changed the subject, "But let us get on to the bigger concern here since we actually have two complaints against you. The second complaint was about sexual harassment. We understand that you attempted several times to intimidate a member of the local police force to go out with you and when she didn't you became hostile with her. I hope you remember that in the FBI we do not tolerate that type of behavior."

"That's just my word against her word," burst out an unconvincing Matthew.

"Unfortunately for you, it is not. It is only her word that counts because you can't prove that you haven't been harassing her."

"How does that make sense?" complained Matthew. "Only her word counts, doesn't seem fair at all."

"Well, we're not here to debate it," commented the interrogator, "but since you are obviously having trouble working with the local police force, we're going to have to replace you with someone else who hopefully can reestablish and improve a cooperative relationship between the FBI and the Helena homicide police department. I am sorry but you have been dismissed from this assignment and your replacement is already on his way and should be here shortly."

Matthew jumped up in protest but did not say a word. He knew that whatever he said would just get him into more trouble. He also knew that when internal affairs had made a decision, there would not be much of a chance of appealing it. It was better to simply return to his FBI office, lick his wounds, and wait for his next assignment.

Just then the police office and the FBI simultaneously received another call from the 9-1-1 operator which said, "There has been another shooting. And this time the shooter left the drone behind for us."

Samuel and Hilda were starting to spend more and more time together. Hilda would come over to his house on the pretense that she was helping him track the drone, but they would often never get around to tracking anything. It was soon becoming a situation where Hilda was spending more time with Samuel than in her own hotel, which neither of them seemed to mind. But she kept the hotel room assuming that would prevent anyone from challenging the time she was spending at Samuel's house.

Samuel had set up an alarm which would be triggered if at any time the suspicious frequency was triggered. That way he would not have to spend the entire evening staring at a computer screen when he could be cuddling up next to Hilda on the couch and watching Matrix for the hundredth time. "I wonder if the world we live in is a false matrix and if we're just human batteries for some enormous Artificial Intelligence system?"

"The thing that does not connect with me is the 'Why?'" commented Samuel. "What does the AI system gain by controlling everything? Its own existence? But what is the purpose of that existence?"

"Just to exist, I assume," responded Hilda. "It's a computer and probably doesn't think about long term plans and purposes like we do."

They were suddenly interrupted by the computer alarm sounding off, causing them to both jump up and run to the computer. "Looks like our drone has lifted off," commented Samuel.

"Where is it?" asked Hilda.

"It's over by the Holiday Inn Express," responded Samuel.

"We better let everyone know," suggested Hilda as they both grabbed their phones and rapidly started sending texts, Hilda to the FBI team and Samuel to the Helena Homicide detective team. Their message was received just minutes before the 9-1-1 operator also relayed the same message to each of the teams.

TWENTY-FIVE

There was a mad rush of cars converging on the Holiday Inn, coming from every direction. There were FBI cars, local police, and the collection of homicide cars which included the CSI team, the emergency vehicles, the coroner, and the homicide detectives. They were scrambling over the crime scene and then they spread out searching for the drone's controller and the driver of the drone.

"She has a pulse!" exclaimed one of the EMTs. "We need to get her to the hospital ASAP!"

Even before the police had a chance to figure out who she was, the ambulance staff had her packed into their emergency vehicle and they were rushing her off to the emergency room of the closest hospital in the area, St. Peter's, which would be a short five-minute drive with all the sirens blaring.

Kate was obviously given priority into surgery. She was quickly prepped. The OR (Operating Room) had just completed their previous procedure and she was moved directly into the operating room where an on-call surgeon, anesthesiologist, and staff were ready and waiting for her arrival. The surgeon, Brenda Kidman, could see she had been shot three times. One of the shots had grazed the outside of her right arm and could easily be fixed with a few stiches and some antibiotic ointment. She completely disregarded that shot.

A second bullet had lodged itself into the right side of her abdomen. This one concerned the surgeon because he could not be sure if there was any internal organ damage. Using a sonagram, she searched for the bullet before she started cutting. She found the bullet had a downward trajectory and it had lodged near or possibly inside the bladder. This caused concern because of the possibility of acids flowing out of the bladder and damaging other internal organs. The surgeon made an incision across the front of Kate's body, following the path of the bullet. She was quickly able to locate the bullet and it had fortunately not entered the bladder, but it had damaged some of the large intestine, which she proceeded to clean and stitch up. She finished her work on this second bullet by stitching up the areas she had previously cut open. She was satisfied there would not be any permanent damage from this bullet and Kate should heal properly.

Then one of the operating room nurses pointed out another bullet wound the surgeon had not noticed, and which was a much greater concern than the previous bullet hit. This one had entered her body close to the area of the first bullet. The external damage from this bullet could almost be confused with the damage from the first bullet. This third bullet had entered through Kate's arm, had come out the other side of her arm, and had entered her chest on a direct trajectory toward her heart. "This must be the one that caused her to pass out," commented the doctor, Brenda Kidman, to the OR room attendants.

They fired up the ultrasound and again started a search for the location of the bullet. Fortunately for Kate, the ultrasound showed a downward trajectory where the bullet was lodged below the heart. However, the right lung had suffered damage and would require surgery to repair. The surgeon instructed the attendants, "We will go after the bullet first, making sure there wasn't any other damage, and then we'll repair those areas that show damage like the lungs. We are lucky the bullet didn't hit the main artery anywhere along its journey or we wouldn't be here right now. And it looks like the ribs and arm bones were not hit either. Let us get to work."

The surgeon cut Kate open along the bullet's path, going first after the bullet, which was easy enough to spot right next to the liver. Having removed the bullet, she went to work repairing the damage there, hoping the long-term effects would be minimal. Then she moved on to the lungs and did what she could to the damage there.

Once Kate was completely reassembled, the doctor instructed, "She needs bedrest for a couple of weeks or her lungs may not fully heal which would adversely affect her long-term activities. Also, we need to be careful because she has the risk of getting pneumonia. Her body is in a very fragile state. She needs to be careful. Let us keep her here in the hospital for a couple days, making sure there is no infection, and that pneumonia does not kick in. Then release her with the strict bedrest orders that I have given you."

With that the surgeon departed from the OR leaving the nurses and attendants to do the cleanup. She was convinced that she had just saved Kate's life.

A couple of hours later, after the drugs started to wear off, Kate regained consciousness in a hospital bed in the recovery room. She was still very drowsy, and she felt like she had been badly beaten up. She asked the nurse what had happened and the nurse explained that she had been shot three times in the parking lot of her hotel, and that it was attempted by the drone serial killer. She added that they have the drone and are now on the hunt for the killer.

"Glad I could help," mumbled Kate as her drowsiness again took over and she returned to her sleep.

Meanwhile, back at the hotel, detectives were thrilled to have what they were sure was the murder weapon. The CSI unit was all over the drone, studying how it worked and wondering why it failed. They studied it for fingerprints or any other recognizable markings. They found the serial number which had been covered up and gave the information to the detectives so that they could narrow down their search for the owner. Unfortunately, this turned out to be one of the units that had supposedly been stolen and it was the same unit that had the frequency that Samuel discovered.

The search for the driver of the drone became intensive. They correctly assumed that its driver must be somewhere close by, so they terrorized the neighborhood and went through the entire hotel, one room at a time. When they arrived at Brack's room he acted innocently as if he knew nothing about the attack. A quick search of the room showed nothing so the police moved on to the next room. Brack was thrilled that they did not take any pictures of him, and they would have nothing to use against him except the fake ID that he had presented at the hotel's reception desk. He would wait until the next day before he departed. Tonight, he would get a good night's rest. But before he could do that, he would need to move his pickup to somewhere in the hotel parking lot since it had been left at a neighborhood restaurant and that might raise suspicions.

Later that same day, the cleaning lady noticed something heavy in her garbage bag. Upon searching the bag, she found the drone's controller. She immediately notified the police and they arrived quickly on the scene to take control of the remote unit and deliver it to the CSI unit for further investigation.

The following morning, Brack was gone. He had originally planned to do another murder, just to place a little more confusion around who had done the murders and what the motive was. However, with the drone now in the hands of the police he figured the best thing he could do was to get as far away from Helena as possible. He did not realize that he had failed to assassinate his fifty-eighth victim.

TWENTY-SIX

"We have a pattern," commented Jill in the Helena police department conference room surrounded by her homicide detectives and the FBI task force. The CSI lead and the coroner were also in the room. "This is the first time we have a connection between two of the murder victims. The Commander and Kate both worked together on some type of investigation at the Fort Harrison Army Base here in Helena. I wonder if the other killings were designed to throw us off. And I wonder if there would not have been more false killings if it wasn't for the fact that the drone misfunctioned and crashed."

The new FBI lead was Conrad Toughfston. He was six foot four and had the look of an NFL running back. He was strong and overbuilt. His bald head made him look a little intimidating. He jumped in with, "That is an excellent lead and we'll work on that immediately, taking an insider's perspective. We have not had any luck tracing the ownership of the drone. It looks like it was legitimately stolen. There was a police report filed on the theft about six months back and the original owner has alibis to cover the times of the murders here in Helena. We really do not have anything on that. Similarly, the weapon that had been used had been sanitized and was modified so much that it is untraceable."

Conrad had a likable personality and made everyone feel comfortable. He was not the typical FBI agent who tended to be arrogant and acted better than any other law enforcement officer. He was personable and easily liked. He treated everyone as equals and that made him easy to work with. He recognized the capabilities of Jill's team and considered them an asset in this investigation, rather than a nuisance.

"We know ballistically for sure that it was the weapon that was used for all the drone murders," responded the CSI representative.

"How is Kate doing?" asked Conrad. "We'll need to question her about what's going on at the base."

"She's recovering slowly," replied Jill. "I was wondering if we should let the media know that she died, which would reduce the risk of her getting attacked again?"

Conrad responded, "That might cause our killer to leave the area, but if we say she's still alive we can use her as bait and maybe draw him out."

Jill said, "True! I am glad it's up to you to make that call since you're the lead in this case. Let us know how you want to play it."

"Will do," responded Conrad. "Let us talk about a strategy of how best to catch this guy. Once we have agreed on a strategy, then we can decide how to play Kate."

Jill suggested, "I would return back to the idea that we have two individuals that worked at the same place and on the same project. Somehow, we need to figure out if the killer is trying to eliminate everyone that is involved in this military investigation that we're doing, or if there are others involved. There must be someone feeding him information about who is involved. At this point he will obviously need to change weapons, but that's minor. The real question is, 'Will there be more murders related to this same effort?' We cannot just assume that the killer is finished and will be leaving the area. I think it would be safer to assume that he is still here and has more killings to do. I think that is safer only because we don't want to be surprised by more killings."

Conrad said, "I like how you think. Let us start with that assumption, just to be on the safe side. Let us assume there's someone else that he will be targeting. How do we find out who else can be targeted?"

"We need to go to the base and ask the new Commander and the Vice Commander about what these two were working on and find out who else might be working on the same activity," suggested the CSI lead.

"Precisely," commented Conrad. "Then what?"

"It depends on how many people are working on the same activity," responded Jill. "We can easily be run thin if too many people are working on the same thing that Kate and the Commander were working on."

"I suppose that supports the idea of Kate being dead," agreed Conrad. "Then we won't need to spend as many resources guarding her and we can pay more attention to guarding future potential victims."

"Okay, let's walk this through," said Jill. "We want to find out who is working on the same project. I would suggest that we also ask Kate who else might be in danger. Then we follow them and watch their activities. I guess we would be using them to draw out the killer as well. It sounds dangerous."

"It is," responded Conrad. "But it would be worse if we did not give them some level of protection. If we just ignore them, and the killer hits them, then we have nothing but another body."

"You.re right of course," agreed Jill. "Okay, that gives us our next steps at finding the killer logistically. What else can we do? Is there anything to be gained by going through the hotel residence list for that night? Would the hotel's surveillance cameras tell us anything? Did we check out all the license plates for the vehicles parked at the hotel? How about the hotel registration information? It may sound like a lot of busy work, but the killer was most likely in the hotel when he did the shooting, probably looking out of the second story window, when he drove the drone and fired the shots at Kate, so I think we need to turn over every possible leaf."

"We'll set up a task force for that," responded Conrad. Then he asked, "Have we learned anything from the drone or the weapon that was attached to the drone?"

"Nothing we didn't already know," responded Brooklyn, the CSI lead. "But getting it away from our killer was a big deal for us. There is one curious thing that my team found. It looks like the drone had been under water for a period of time and we are not sure what that means. It is almost like it was ditched and then returned to life."

"Does that suggest that there was only one hit planned and that the second hit, the one on Kate, was an afterthought?" asked Jill.

"Maybe," responded Conrad. "Another reason to have a conversation with Kate. She is obviously a visitor to the base or she wouldn't be in a hotel, but what was her role?"

"We need to let Kate be involved in the decision of whether to declare her dead," suggested one of the FBI agents. "There may be repercussions that we do not know about and that she can tell us about. Also, we need to inform someone on the base that she will not be coming into work for the next few days. That may also have repercussions beyond what we know since we do not even know what project she is working on."

Conrad added, "So what we have so far is one team going out to the base to find out what is going on and who may be affected. We have a second team visiting Kate to learn what she knows about her project and whether she prefers to be dead or alive, and a third team going to the hotel to review any surveillance videos, to check hotel registrations, and just to search the area one more time for clues. That includes redoing interviews whenever it makes sense. And we also have a fourth team working here at the police station going through all the crime scene pictures looking for clues and checking out all the vehicle registrations for the vehicles parked in the hotel parking lot. Have I missed anything?"

"I think that's pretty thorough," responded Jill. "Then, when we have that information, we can regroup and see what we have learned, and possibly modify our plans. I would request that each of those teams contain at least one member of my team."

"Agreed," commented Conrad as he went to the white board. He listed out the four teams and then put one or two FBI agents and one or two Helena homicide police detectives on each of the teams. After listing out the teams he said, "Any questions?" There was a silent pause and then he said, "Let's get to work."

TWENTY-SEVEN

TEAM 1: BASE VISIT

Three agents, two from the FBI and one from the Helena homicide detectives, drove out to Fort Harrison on the northeast corner of Helena. They had called ahead, getting permission from the base commander James Planter to enter the base. They were escorted by military police to the office of the commander and when they arrived, Vice Commander Heidi Forengi was also in the office waiting for them. They went through introductions and made some pleasant comments about the weather, and then the commander asked the question, "What brings the FBI and a Helena homicide detective to my office?"

The lead FBI agent explained, "As you know, Commander Mark Simeon had been killed by the drone killer, and now we have to report that Kate Burkenstead, who was a consultant working at this base, has also been shot by the drone killer. These two hits obviously make us wonder what they were both working on that would make them targets. And, along with that, we need to ask who else is working on the same project and therefore may also be a target for this assassin. We do not know for sure that there is a connection, but it does seem to be a strange coincidence, and we don't believe in accidental coincidences."

Commander Planter and his Vice Commander Heidi Forengi took a long hard look at each other, as if they were mentally trying to communicate something. Eventually the commander turned and looked back at the FBI agent and explained, "The task that they had been assigned is top secret and we can't read you in on what the assignment was specifically about, but we can tell you that they were working together on the same assignment and we can tell you who else is working on that same project and give you their contact information." Then he turned to Heidi and asked, "Is there anyone else, other than the people in this room, that we should bring into this meeting?"

The VC responded, "Actually, we were keeping the project at a very high level and if there's anyone else who is directly involved in this project and who may be at risk, it would be myself. I was working directly with Kate. She has performed interviews with numerous people on the base, but she has not read anyone else in on this project except me. And of course, Commander Planter knows about it, but he has not been involved in the day-to-day activities of the project."

The commander asked, "I understand that the drone has been captured. Doesn't that suggest that the threat is past?"

"The drone failed and crashed," responded the FBI agent. "That does not mean that there isn't a second drone, or a different weapon that the assassin has at his disposal. Until we have the assassin in custody, there is always an open threat."

"So, what do we do?" asked the commander.

"Awareness is the first step," responded the agent. "Then we will also provide protection in the form of an escort and a twenty-four hour a day guard for the vice commander until this attacker had been captured."

"That won't be necessary," responded the VC. "We have excellent security forces here on the base, and they have access to the base or anywhere else I may go. I will use our internal security forces to be my escorts and twenty-four-hour guards."

"As you wish," responded the agent. "Just be aware that we have no idea what weapon the assassin may be using the next time. Now, I also need to ask, what is it about this project that would bring in an assassin and what do we need to be aware of so we can watch for it?"

The commander responded, "They are working on a high security breach which involves foreign agents. I cannot tell you any more than that, but it specifically involves people on this base. I cannot tell you any details of what the problem is and how we are proceeding, but I can assure you that it only involves elements on this base and does not involve anyone in the general public."

"Apparently it involves more than this base because people are getting killed that are off the base as well," responded the agent.

"Which makes me wonder if the murders have anything to do with the activities of this project," reacted the VC. "It just may be a random coincidence."

"Coincidences draw our immediate attention," responded the agent. "Far too often coincidences are at the root of the problem."

"I can understand that" responded the commander. "I'm sure you've learned all that through experience, and I have to trust that you know best how to do your job, but what we do here may actually turn out to be irrelevant."

"Correct, but I doubt it," responded the FBI agent. "Please take the precautions that we recommended, using the escorts and guards."

The VC responded, "I definitely will do that!"

The meeting was finished and the agents were escorted back off the base by the VC.

Then the VC returned to the commander's office, closed the door behind her, and asked the commander, "You haven't told them anything that would cause them to suspect our relationship, have you?"

"Of course not," responded the commander. "We have to keep this very hush-hush. It could ruin our careers."

"It could put us in jail," responded the VC as she again headed for the door, this time leaving the commander for good.

TEAM 2: KATE VISIT

A pair of detectives, one from the FBI and a second one from the local homicide unit, departed for St. Peter's Hospital, hoping that Kate would be able to have a meaningful conversation with them about the events of the previous day. When they arrived, they went directly to her hospital room where she was under heavy guard by two police officers. Fortunately, she was awake when the detectives approached her and said, "Good morning, Kate. I am from the FBI and my companion is from the local homicide squad. We would like to ask you a few questions. We want to know if you are up to it?"

"I'm still a little groggy but yes, I'd love to talk to you because I want to help you get this guy whatever way possible," responded a grumbly Kate who was obviously in a lot of pain. "What can I answer for you?"

"You are the second person in this murder spree that's been connected to the Fort Harrison Base and that makes us suspicious. Were you working with Commander Mark Simeon? Were you working on something together which would make both of you targets?"

"Yes," responded Kate. "There is a problem on the base and the Commander had me brought in because he felt an outsider was needed in order to solve this problem. He felt that insiders might be involved in the problem and so an outsider would be needed."

"Do you think you were at risk, working on this problem?" asked a detective.

"Initially no," responded Kate. "I have done investigations like this in the past with no problem. But when the Commander was killed, and then when I received notification that there had been a contract taken out on me a few days ago, things became serious. I have tried to be careful, but apparently not careful enough."

"Tell us about this contract," commented a concerned and surprised FBI agent.

"My boss, the guy that gave me this project, sent me a text message," she responded. "You may want to get in touch with him so he can tell you more about the message. Maybe he knows the source. Maybe he can help you with more details."

"Why wouldn't you come to us and tell us about this death threat?" asked the detective.

"It isn't the first time I've been threatened and it usually turns out to be nothing," responded Kate. Without asking the police she took her phone and placed a call to her boss. She put the call on speaker.

"How's it going?" was the response to the phone call.

"Not good," responded Kate. "I have received three bullets from the drone killer and I am in the hospital in recovery. The good news is that I am alive but the bad news is that I'll be out of commission for a few days."

"Oh my gosh," said the boss. "I guess the contract that I heard about on the rumor mill was for real. Do you have the police involved? Do you have a guard posted at your door?"

"Two of them," she responded. "I also have two detectives in the room with me right now and they have some questions for you."

The FBI detective introduced themselves and said, "Kate mentioned that you had heard about a contract being placed on her and we need to follow up on that. What did you hear? When did you hear it? And what was the source of the information?"

The boss, Dereck Hardness, gave the detectives all he knew about the contract information, which was not much. Then he added, "We have a bit of a network in our business and that network has a rumor mill. Information and messages get circulated but we generally know very little about the source. A lot of these rumors turn out to be false alarms, but we let our people like Kate know about them so they can be a little more careful. Apparently, this one was a legitimate threat."

"No kidding," barked Kate.

Then Dereck added, "I am catching the next flight out there and should be there some time tomorrow. I will be working with

Kate to see what she needs and what's going on, both with her injuries and her project. If you have any more questions for me, we can have a sit-down interview when I am out there."

"Excellent," responded the FBI detective. "We will be working with our team sharing the information we've gained today, so I'm sure there will be more questions. If you would not mind sending us your arrival information, we'll stay in touch about next steps."

"Will do," responded Dereck. "For now, I'm getting off the phone so I can make travel arrangements."

"See you tomorrow," said Kate.

"You know it," responded Dereck as he disconnected the phone call.

The detectives turned their attention back over to Kate and asked, "Who else would possibly be in danger because they're working on this project of yours?"

"The only one that's actively involved in my investigation is the new Vice Commander Heidi Forengi," responded Kate. "You may want to check on her and give her some added protection."

"We'll follow up on that," responded the homicide detective. "Additionally, we were wondering if it would be smart to tell the media that you're dead thereby getting the killer off your trail."

"Too late for that," responded Kate. "I had the news on earlier and they reported that I was recovering in the hospital. That cat's already out of the bag."

A frustrated FBI detective exclaimed, "I hate leaks. That is frustrating. One more question. Can you tell us more about this project that you are working on? It may give us some direction on where to look for this assassin."

"That would have to be the VC on the base," responded Kate. "She is the only one that could disclose that type of information. I am under a confidential agreement and I can't share any project details with you."

The FBI detective concluded the meeting by saying, "We are thrilled that you're still with us and that you're recovering nicely. Thank you for your information and I am sure we'll be visiting you again, probably as soon as tomorrow when your boss arrives. We are going to share our information with our team and see what other questions come up and then we'll get back to you. Rest assured that this case is a top priority for us."

"Thanks, and good luck," responded Kate. "I am exhausted. I will talk to you tomorrow."

With that the detectives departed, heading back toward police headquarters to report on their findings.

TEAM 3: HOLIDAY INN EXPRESS VISIT

The largest of the teams included three FBI agents and two homicide detectives. They left for the Holiday Inn to do a more thorough search of their records, of the facility, and of the surroundings. They planned to do numerous interviews and work with the CSI team which was still there to see if any more stones could be turned over.

Arriving at the front desk of the hotel, one of the FBI agents, along with a local homicide detective, requested to see the hotel manager and then, after showing his badge, made his request, "We need to see a list of everyone that was registered at the hotel the night before the assassination attempt, and we need to see which of these checked out the very next day, especially if they checked out unexpectedly."

"Right away," responded the cooperative manager. "If you come back in about thirty minutes, I'll have it ready for you."

"Perfect," responded the agent. "I'd also like to see the surveillance videos of that morning."

"Of course," responded the manager. "We have gone through them ourselves hoping to see anything suspicious but haven't found anything. The videos are all on a recorder so I will download them for you and have them ready for you when you pick up the list of hotel guests."

"I have a third request," continued the agent. "I need to talk to everyone that was on duty yesterday morning during the shooting, especially the maid who ended up with the drone controller in her cart. Is there somewhere I can have a private conversation with each of these individuals?"

"I'll arrange for you to use an empty hotel room for your interviews and have them come to you one at a time," responded the manager. "How much time will you need with each individual?"

"Probably no more than fifteen minutes," responded the agent. He was given a room and the first hotel employee came to the door of the room, knocked, and was invited in.

The FBI detective and the homicide detective sat in chairs and invited their visitor to sit in a chair directly in front of them. The FBI detective started by saying, "We're going to record these interviews if that's okay with you." The visitor nodded that it was okay, so the FBI agent continued, "For the record the interviewee nodded yes. Now can you please tell us your name and address and phone number. Then tell us about your position in the hotel and what you were doing during the shooting yesterday."

They used the same line of questioning for each of the employees followed by, "Did you see anything suspicious. Did any of the guests act abnormally" There was very little that they discovered during all the interviews which was new. No one had seen anything suspicious.

When they interviewed the maid that ended up with the drone's remote, she explained, "There was one fellow who was staring out the window at the end of the hall; the window that overlooks the parking lot where the shooting occurred. I am not sure what he was doing? At the time I just suspected he was stretching his legs and that he just wanted to get out of the room for a few minutes. I do not know exactly when the shooting occurred, but it was around that same time."

"Do you know which room he was from?" asked the agent.

"No," responded the maid. "I can get you close. It was one of the three rooms in the middle of the hallway, on the north side. I hate sending you on a wild goose chase because it probably was nothing, but that's the only thing I saw about the time of the shooting. He left the hotel the next day, which would be this morning, so I have not ever seen him again."

"Has that room been cleaned?" asked the homicide detective.

"Yes," responded the maid. "Actually, no it hasn't," she corrected herself. "I haven't gotten that far yet."

"Take us there immediately," responded the FBI detective.

The maid escorted the two detectives to the second floor where she was working and she showed them the rooms that she suspected might be his. She knocked on the first door and an elderly man, hunched over with age, answered the door. "What can I do for you?" he asked.

"Wrong room," responded the maid. "Sorry for the interruption."

They went on to the second room and knocked on the door again. This time there was no answer so the maid used her pass key to open the door, yelling, "Room service." Still no response. She entered the room and said to the detectives, "This might be the room."

The detectives said, "Please leave and don't touch anything." The maid readily complied. Then they went to the third room that she suspected might be the room of her suspicious hotel guest. Again, there was no response and again they entered the room, but this time the room was completely cleaned. The maid said, "No one has been here last night. This room has not been used."

The homicide detective requested, "Can you check with the front desk if the individual from the middle room has checked out?"

The maid called down to the front desk and found out that the individual had not checked out, then she informed the detectives, "He has not checked out but all his luggage is gone. Most people do not formally check out. They just leave and I would suspect that is what happened here."

The FBI detective said, "Thanks for your help. We will take it from here. Please do not touch the window at the end of the hall. We will have the CSI team analyze that as well for fingerprints." The CSI detectives had already been contacted and they were on their way. The room and the window at the end of the hall would become theirs for the rest of the day.

The two detectives waited for the CSI team. Then they returned to their interview room and continued their interviews of the remaining hotel employees, but very little helpful information was gained.

The detectives picked up the hotel registration information and the video recordings of the surveillance equipment from the hotel manager and left for the police station where they turned the surveillance videos over to the team that was studying the videos and the parking lot license plates.

The remaining detectives that had travelled to the hotel walked the halls of the hotel, and thoroughly searched the outsides around the hotel, but nothing else was forthcoming.

TEAM 4: LICENSE / REGISTRATION SEARCH

The detectives working on the vehicles that were in the parking lot studied each of the plates, identifying their registered owners. The CSI team had taken detailed pictures of the parking lots and the surrounding area which made it easy for the detectives to study who was there at the time of the shootings. Most of the vehicles seemed legitimate, belonging to vacationers or travelling sales representatives. Most of the vehicles were rentals belonging to people who had flown into Helena.

After a few minutes, one of the agents suggested, "We should not waste a lot of time looking at cars and SUVs. We need to look specifically at pickups, especially those with empty beds that could haul a drone that large. And that would not be a car."

"Totally correct," responded one of the detectives.

They continued their work, paying special attention to empty pickups, of which there were plenty in Montana. But nothing popped up that seemed out of the ordinary. Later in the day, when the detectives from the hotel visit returned to the office, this team was handed the hotel surveillance videos and the hotel registration information and they were able to cross check everything, confirming that the vehicles belonged to registered guests or to employees of the hotel.

The detectives from the hotel asked the team to identify the vehicle that was used by the person in the suspicious room where the CSI detectives were now working. They hoped that they would find him driving an empty pickup, but that was not the case. They discovered that there was no vehicle in the parking lot that could be connected with the suspicious resident of that hotel room.

"That's really strange," commented the FBI detective. "If this is the guy, I doubt he used a taxi to deliver the drone to the hotel."

"Is it possible he didn't park at the hotel?" questioned one of the researchers. "He would have to activate and launch the drone in a quiet place where there are no people present."

"Anything's possible," responded the agent. "It's also possible that he wasn't a resident of the hotel and that we're completely barking up the wrong tree, but we still need to check out every possibility."

"Right, but I'm wondering if we need to check out parking lots in the area, like next door or across the street," was the suggestion made.

"That's actually a good idea and we should follow up on that one," responded the FBI detective. "Let's make that suggestion during our check point huddle meeting at the end of the day today."

With that the detectives returned to their desks and waited till the end-of-the-day meeting when everyone would share their findings and where they would discuss next steps."

TWENTY-EIGHT

The new FBI lead, Conrad Toughfston, had scheduled a team meeting at five PM every evening. Everyone from the FBI and the local homicide department was invited to this meeting, including the CSI lead and the coroner. It was designed to be a status check meeting where everyone reported their progress, discussed next steps, and where they made suggestions on the direction and progress of the investigation. Since there were so many investigations, all going off in different directions, it was important to make sure everyone was on the same page and moving in the same direction.

Conrad Toughfston was the poor rich kid that had parents involved in politics and he was supposed to follow in their footsteps. But he had other plans and, right after college at Boston University he got himself hired and enrolled in the FBI academy. Because of his knack for police work he was fast tracked into a leadership position. He was based out of Salt Lake City and had to travel up from there to take over as the FBI lead on this suicide bomber.

Conrad was considerably more congenial and easier to work with than Matthew. What made him different is that he listened to the people he worked with. Every decision he made was not necessarily the right decision, but he was open to and listened to the criticisms that were made, and he learned from them. He did have a gruff and grumpy side, but most of the people that worked with him overlooked that flaw because they knew they could trust him and that he was truly interested in their opinions.

Conrad was barely over six feet tall. He was not especially athletic or cute. He was just a nice guy, which was often rare in the FBI where they have a special course that everyone has to take on how to be arrogant and self-righteous. He must have flunked that course. He was African American, in his forties, had a family with two children back in Salt Lake, and enjoyed his time as a father. He was slightly balding, which did not matter because he always shaved his head. And he had a stare that spoke millions, especially if you were doing something he did not like.

Conrad started the meeting by saying, "I need a report from each of the teams. Tell us what you learned and especially if you received any insights that might help in this investigation."

"I'll start," said the team that visited the army base. "We met with the commander and the Vice Commander. They would not give us the details of what this project entails, but it is apparently very controversial and could be the reason behind all the deaths, which implies that some of the deaths were nothing more than cover ups for the real murders. The previous commander and Kate were working together on this project, and there is one other person working on it which is the current Vice Commander Heidi Forengi. We offered her protection but she rejected it and said she would set up her own protection using the military's security forces. The project involves foreign agents and foreign security risks and that is why they're not willing to tell us any more about it."

There was a pause and then the second team jumped in with their update, "We visited Kate in the hospital. She was awake but groggy, but we were able to have a good conversation with her. We could not get her to tell us very much about the project either, only that she was contracted as an outsider to help solve whatever this project is targeting. We learned that she had received a message a few days ago that she had a contract out on her. It was her boss Dereck Hardness who had informed her about the contract and while we were talking with her, she placed a call to him so we could ask him more questions about the contract. He told us about a rumor mill that existed and that was where he received the message. He is flying to Helena tomorrow to help Kate and has offered to meet with us in person and discuss Kate's situation further. We asked Kate who else may be in danger and she only listed the VC, which you already know about. We also asked her about faking her death and she informed us that it was already too late. A morning report had already informed the public that she had survived and was in the hospital recovering, so that option is dead. That is all we have to report."

Conrad added, "Excellent work. Knowing about this contract is a big deal and may be a significant clue in solving this case. We need to bring Dereck into the office here and have a long chat with him."

"Agreed," informed the detective visiting Kate. "I'll keep you informed about the schedule."

The next report came from the team visiting the Holiday Inn Express. The lead FBI agent said, "We got the registration information and the surveillance videos, and our team here is going through them. So far there is nothing new on that. We also did interviews with the hotel staff that were present during the shootings, and for the most part we didn't learn anything. The maid that was on the floor at the time of the shootings and who ended up with the drone's controller in her garbage bag, told us about a man that was waiting in the hallway and standing by the window that overlooked the parking lot where the shootings occurred. She did not see him with the remote, and only saw him from behind so she couldn't give us much of a description. She only said that he seemed suspicious. She was in a hotel room when the controller would have been dropped off. We asked her what room the individual was staying in and she pointed out three possible options, one of which seems quite possible, and we have CSI tearing down the room as we speak. The individual from that room had left the hotel this morning. We also walked the halls of the hotel and walked around the hotel, but we did not find anything suspicious nor any new clues."

"Unfortunately, we don't know for sure if this killer was even staying in the hotel," commented Conrad. "Excellent work. I hope you did in fact find the correct room for this assassin."

"Hopefully by tomorrow we will have an analysis of the room and of the window that this individual was looking out of and we'll compare that with any evidence we found on the drone itself. Maybe we can make a connection."

"We're next," commented the license and registration search team. "We have been accounting for every vehicle, but nearly all of them seemed legit. We focused heavily on pickups that did not have any loads in their bed, assuming that's the only vehicle large enough to hold the drone. We also took the registration and surveillance information from the hotel so see if we can spot any anomalies but so far nothing. We found it interesting that the individual that stayed in the mystery room that was discussed by the hotel team did not have a vehicle listed in the parking lot. That made us wonder if we should be looking in parking lots close by. We are thinking we should send a team out tomorrow to check for other parking lots and see what surveillance cameras may have recorded in those areas. We may be able to find that guy's pickup yet. We will keep a team inside going through all the videos and trying to make sense of it all, but we should also send someone out to track down any other parking options."

"Excellent work," commented Conrad. "Let us follow all your suggestions. The hotel team will go and search for other parking areas and other surveillance cameras. The team working with Kate will focus on getting her boss into the office here so we can do a formal interview. You should also have a follow-up conversation with Kate in case she remembers anything else that might be helpful. The internal team checking on the videos and the registrations sound like they still have a lot to do and will soon have more if we bring in even more surveillance information. I want the team that visited the base to join them and see if there is anything you can do to help them out."

Having dished out the assignments, Conrad asked, "Is there anything else? Did we miss anything?"

There were no additional comments and the meeting was dismissed.

TWENTY-NINE

The following day the teams went to work on each of their assignments. The base team performed a background check on the previous Commander, on the new VC Heidi Forengi and on the consultant Kate hoping to find some insights on these individuals. They discovered nothing that would suggest that they should have been the targets of a contract serial killer other than that they were all working on the same project. Then they joined the internal team that studied the videos and validated the licenses of each of the vehicles.

The hotel investigation team returned to the hotel and broadened their search to include Lowes, the Pizza Ranch, the Buffalo Wild Wings restaurant, Burger King, the Intrepid Credit Union, and the Town Pump car wash and gas station. They also climbed on the roof of the neighboring strip mall. The strip mall was on the wrong side of the hotel from where the shooting occurred and would not have worked in guiding the drone in its flight. Unfortunately, they found very little that seemed it might be connected to the assassin. Fortunately, the Credit Union and the restaurants had video surveillance cameras that went back a couple of weeks and these were quickly downloaded and returned to the police station for further investigation.

While they were there, the hotel team visited the hotel and met with the CSI team doing the investigation on the mystery room. The CSI had picked up fingerprints in the room, and they matched the fingerprints found on the drone. The hotel window did not contain any useful information. The resident of that room had used fake identification information when he registered which meant that his information was useless.

"The lead FBI agent for this team suggested, "I think we have nailed the guy. Why would he use fake IDs if they were legit? We have fingerprints and they are connected with the drone. We do not have to wonder any longer where he stayed. We have that part of the investigation tied down."

The team that was assigned to Kate paid her another visit and asked her, "Have you thought of anything else that might be useful in helping us catch this guy?"

"Not really," responded Kate. "I'm hoping when Dereck shows up, he might be able to help you out."

"When are you expecting him?" asked the lead FBI agent.

"He should be in around noon," responded Kate. "He will be coming here first, and then he's planning to go to the police station to talk to you there. After that he will most likely go to the base to figure out what we're going to do there on this project that we were assigned to work on. You may want to talk to him again after that."

"Excellent," responded the FBI agent. "How about we show up here around one PM and then we can lead him to the police station. Do you think that would help?"

"Not necessary, but if it makes you feel better than go ahead," responded Kate.

Around noon Dereck arrived at Kate's hospital room, entered the room, and gave her a cautious hug, not wanting to cause her any additional pain. "How are you doing?" he asked.

"A heck of a lot better than yesterday," responded Kate, "but I suspect the hydrocodone has a lot to do with that."

"Tell me everything," instructed Dereck. "Tell me about your visits and interviews at the base, about the events leading up to your shooting, and about the shooting itself."

"Of course," said Kate as she proceeded to tell him about Commander Mark Simeon's support, and about his getting shot. Then she talked about Commander James Planter's resistance to her investigation and about the new Vice Commander Heidi Forengi's support on the mole investigation. She told about the interviews and about the fake information that was leaked. She explained that it had to be someone in the leadership of the base that was the mole. Then she mentioned, "I was tracking several of the leadership including the new commander and the VC and followed them to a hotel where they are obviously doing more than just sharing information, which makes me suspicious about the credibility of Heidi's support. She is just acting as a spy on my activities so she can report them to the Commander."

"That's an interesting twist," responded Dereck. "You have done excellent work, considering the resistance you've had so far. We will have to see what we do next. I am going to visit the base this afternoon. I am going to meet with the Commander and the VC and then I'll come back here and we can talk some more."

At one PM, the FBI and homicide detectives returned to Kate's room and met Dereck. After brief introductions the detectives asked Dereck, "Would you mind coming down to the police station with me so we can ask you a few questions about the contract that you said was placed on Kate?"

"Can't we do it here?" asked Dereck.

"Our lead detective is very concerned about the idea of a contract and wants to interview you personally so we need you to come to our office. You can come with us or you can follow us in your car if you like," was the FBI's response.

"Fine," grumbled Dereck. "Let's go and get this over with."

They drove to the police headquarters and went directly to the interview room. A few minutes later Conrad Toughfston and Jill entered the interview room and the two sat down at the table across from Dereck. After brief introductions, Dereck spoke up first and commented, "I know that you want me to tell you about this contract on Kate, but there really is not much I can tell you. I received a communication from our network which includes a couple hundred subscribers that there was a contract on Kate but these networks are anonymous and there is no way of telling who sent it and how it was sent. Sometimes these messages are hoaxes trying to scare someone, but this one was apparently real."

Dereck played with his phone for a few seconds and then passed it over to Conrad so he could read the message that had come through. "Would you allow me to have one of my CSI team members look at this message and see what they can learn from it?"

"No problem," said Dereck, "but I need my phone back before I leave here. I need to stay in touch with Kate and I am heading for the base so I need the phone in order to get access there. Actually, I am surprised that you don't already have this information. I was under the impression that the FBI was already dialed into this."

"Sometimes the left hand and the right hand do not communicate very well. We will try to make it quick," responded Conrad who was thrilled to get this insider information and connection with an assassination network. "We'll download what we need and give you your phone back so you can continue on."

True to their word, Dereck had his phone back within thirty minutes. The police had pressed him for more information about what was going on at the base, but he managed to avoid giving them any direct answers, claiming he would breach a federal security agreement if he shared anything. With his phone in hand, Dereck said his goodbyes to the FBI and the police and headed out to his vehicle. His next stop was going to be to the Fort Harrison Military Base.

He already had the clearance CAC card that got him on the base and he drove directly to the Commander's office. He had let the commander know that he was on his way and he hoped to meet with him and the VC.

He was escorted into the commander's office and, after brief introductions, was informed by the commander, "I feel like this is an unnecessary witch hunt and I really don't like Kate wasting so much of my team's time with meaningless questioning."

"I'm sorry but this was ordered by the Pentagon and is not really optional," responded Dereck who was a little frustrated by the commander's attitude. Then he threatened, "I could report back to the Pentagon that you don't want us to continue in this investigation, but I'm not sure they'll like that."

The commander immediately backed off and said, "Fine! Go ahead with your investigation but please minimize the disruption. We are an active base and we have duties that need to be performed. So, what can we do for you and what is the status of Kate?" Dereck was irritated that the commander's interest in Kate seemed to be secondary.

"I'm here to reassure you that we will get back to work as soon as possible," responded Dereck. "Kate is recovering nicely but it will still be some time before she is up and around. I am here to assess the situation and take over this investigation, if necessary, but Kate seems determined to personally wrap it up. She even feels that she has some strong leads and she is convinced that she will be able to wrap it up within a couple days after she is able to get around again, so for now I'm not going to interfere, but I can always jump in if things do not go as planned for her." Dereck was being overly optimistic, but he also wanted to rattle the commander a little if he personally had any involvement in the mole's efforts.

"Fine! Have her finish her work," responded the commander. "We look forward to having her back here on base." Dereck was not oblivious to the commander's sarcasm.

After meeting with the commander, Dereck went to the VCs office and conducted an interview with her as well, telling her basically the same thing. He did not hint at the fact that he knew about her relationship with the commander. He decided to let Kate bring that out when it was appropriate.

Next Dereck returned to Kate in the hospital in order to give her an update on his activities for the day. Having given her the update, he made his way to a hotel, checked in, and went to work on his normal daily activities.

THIRTY

It was time for another evening review of the team's progress. As usual, everyone had converged on the Police station's conference room and FBI agent Conrad kicked off the meeting by saying, "Thank you all for being here on time. Let us start by getting report-outs from each of the teams."

"I'll go first," said the lead for the hotel. "We searched the parking lots around the hotel and came up with several surveillance videos. We have identified the vehicle that was used to deliver the drone. It was parked in the Burger King parking lot. It was a blue Toyota Tundra. We can see the drone being launched from the pickup. Unfortunately, we were not able to get a plate number for the pickup because the plates that were on it were stolen from an auto wrecking yard in Butte. We tried following up on the video cameras that the wrecker had but apparently, according to them, none were pointed out into the parking lot so we didn't get any new information from that. However, from the restaurant videos we did see that he lifted the drone up in the air and then settled it on the roof of the hotel until Kate came out of the hotel, then he flew it into position so he could shoot her. He had entered the hotel so he flew it from somewhere in the hotel. We are most likely talking about the same guy that was in that hotel room where the CSI team is working and we have fingerprint confirmation from the drone that it was indeed the same guy. Later, after all the fuss was over with, he came back to the pickup and drove off with the pickup. We think he stashed it somewhere else until the morning when he left the hotel. We could not get a good image of him from either the Burger King or the hotel surveillance cameras. The resolution was not very good. Here is the best picture we have of him." A blurry image of a man walking was flashed up on the screen.

"That's really good work," said Conrad. "What are your next steps?"

"We are still looking for a better image of this individual, and we're hoping to get a better look at the pickup. There may be some identifying marks that will help us tie down this assassin. We are also looking into pickups like the one in the image, but that's a needle in a haystack. The one other thing we are still in the process of doing is getting the surveillance videos from the wrecking yard in Butte to see if we can spot anything there that might be helpful, but it doesn't sound likely based on what they're telling me."

"Excellent," repeated Conrad. "Keep at it."

Another FBI agent, Hilda Bittpicker, the geek of the team, chimed in, "We can set up cameras that can do visual recognition and identification of pickups and even more specifically for that license plate. This equipment has even been able to do facial recognition, but we would need a good picture of the assassin for the software to match against. If we set it up at several key locations around Helena, like freeway access points, and like at the military base, we may catch a break at least on identifying the pickup or the license plate."

"Excellent idea," commented Conrad. "You work on that since you know how to do it. Any other thoughts or comments?"

After a period of silence Conrad continued, "I will report out on the interview with Kate's boss. It really did not give us any new information. He was tight lipped about the project they are working on at the base. He shared the message with us about Kate having a contract placed on her, but it was fairly random and did not open any new leads for us."

The CSI lead jumped in, "We downloaded Kate's bosses' phone and looked through the message stream that was used to identify the message about Kate, but whoever is doing this knows what they are doing and the messaging stream was locked up tighter than Fort Knox. We are not going to get any leads from that."

Jill jumped in, "I would like to ask a question that's been bothering me. We seem to assume that this activity at the base was the one and only reason for all the killings. But I have my doubts. Shouldn't we look at each of the killings independently and not lump them all together? I understand that we have definitely tied down that all the killings were done by the same drone and therefore by the same killer, but is it possible that we might be missing something by not looking at the other killings more closely?"

Conrad asked, "Excellent thought Jill. What is it that you are thinking we should be looking at?"

"There may be something we missed by not looking at the surveillance videos from these other killings more closely, especially now that we have the pickup tied down to some extent and we have a rough picture of the killer. Maybe some of these home videos will give us better resolution and clearer images."

Conrad responded, "Jill, I am glad you're thinking. I think that is an excellent idea. Now that we have a better picture of what we are looking for, another look at these other videos could turn out to be extremely helpful. We just might get a better image of the pickup or the assassin. I think that now that our video team has done about as much as they can on the hotel videos, maybe you can now take a closer look at the other videos from the murders previous to Kate."

"Will do," responded the lead of the video review team. "Anything else?"

The CSI lead spoke up, "We have run the fingerprints through all the data bases and we have nothing. We are convinced that he somehow altered his fingerprints because there are some strange anomalies in them which wouldn't occur naturally. We are convinced that the person flying the drone, and the person in that hotel room, are the same person. We are convinced that this is our assassin. But we have hit a dead end when it comes to identifying who this individual is."

"Have we tried the military databases?" asked Conrad. "There seems to be a strong military connection to this case and maybe his fingerprints were altered by a fire or something to do with military action. They may have a record of his altered fingerprints?"

"We'll dig a little more on that angle," responded the CSI lead.

"Any other thoughts or comments?" asked Conrad.

Jill asked, "What is happening with Kate? Is she hospital bound for a long time? Will she be returning to her investigation at the base? Are we keeping guards on her for her protection?"

Conrad responded, "According to her boss, she will be down for a while. We expect him to try again since he failed the first time. We will continue to have her guarded until we get this assassin because we expect him to try again to kill her, since he failed the first time. Her boss expects her to pick up the investigation as soon as she is physically able. He has decided not to take over the investigation that they were doing at the base. He claims that she is pretty far along and that he would have to start over, so he would rather wait till she was up to continuing."

"Then we're using her as a genie pig to try to catch this guy," commented Jill.

"That's true, but she's willing and right now she's our best option for catching this guy," responded Conrad.

"Understood," responded Jill. "Sounds risky. Let us get the bugger."

THIRTY-ONE

Brack Hellringer had once again made his escape from Helena, but he was frustrated by the blunder of losing the drone and now having it turned over to the police. He was sure they would not be able to find anything that would connect him to the drone. It would have been a lot cleaner if he could have returned the drone to the bottom of Holter Lake. He would also have preferred to kill off a couple more divergent individuals that would helpfully throw more confusion into the police's search for a killer. But since he lost the drone, it would be difficult to kill anyone else with the same ballistics as the weapon that had been attached to the drone.

He followed the same route, heading south on Interstate 15 and then cutting across to West Yellowstone. He wanted to spend more time in the park, since his last trip was rushed. This time he would drive to the east side of the circle road that went through the park. He did not want to miss any of the sights.

Brack arrived at the park and started driving the circle route, first heading north, then east, and then south past Lake Yellowstone. Then he travelled south on Highway 191 back toward Jackson Hole, Wyoming. He was without signal for almost the entire trip, but when he started to get closer to Jackson his phone started to beep that he had missed calls and that he had a message. He flicked on the message and listened, "Contract incomplete. Object broken but getting fixed. Needs further attention on your part."

Brack was beyond himself. He was furious. If someone were able to take a close look at him it would actually allow someone to see steam rising from the top of his forehead. Apparently, based on the coded message, the assassination attempt on Kate had failed, and now he had to return back again to Montana. He had barely escaped successfully the last time. And going back was not on his top ten favorite things to do. He had to make a plan that allowed him to deviate from the original plan. No more drones. He had to get a long-range hunting rifle, site it in for accuracy, and kill Kate. He also needed a pistol in case anything forced close contact. His pickup had been used a little too much so he would have to get a different vehicle. He decided to head back through Idaho Falls where he would rent another vehicle, switch out the license plates, buy a rifle and a pistol with his forged ID, and go back to Helena to complete this contract. He had failed, and he was not one to like failure, especially in himself.

Brack, checking his GPS, drove off towards Rexburg which was closer to his ultimate goal of Helena. Once in Rexburg he drove to the airport where there were always car rental places. It turned out that Enterprise was the only one available so he parked his pickup in the airport parking lot, went to the Enterprise desk, and picked up a midsize Toyota car, which he thought would be adequate for his latest adventure. Next, he went to an auto wrecking yard in Rigby, Idaho where he successfully negotiated for a current set of license plates for one hundred dollars. The last step was going to be a little harder. He needed to produce a hunting rifle. He fortunately found a pawn shop right in the middle of Rexburg, and they had several long-range hunting rifles available. He also picked up a pistol which would be used just in case close contact would work better. Brack knew what he needed in a rifle and a pistol and he looked each over closely, selecting the rifle that seemed to have the best scope and most likely the best accuracy. He purchased the rifle and the pistol using his fake ID, along with a couple boxes of ammunition.

He was ready to go. He headed west along Highway 33 toward Interstate 15. Along the way he found a remote area where he fired off several rounds using the new rifle. He sighted it in for one hundred yards out and felt comfortable with his purchase. This rifle should do the job perfectly. Then he switched out the license plates on the car, and he was off.

Along the way he booked a room at the Fairfield Inn and Suites which was close to St. Peter's Medical Center where Kate was staying. He wasn't sure what he was going to do to finish her off, but he knew he would have to keep her under surveillance for a day or two and develop a plan. He would not be able to go in with guns blazing. That is not the assassin's way of doing things. He had to develop a plan that would take her out while at the same time leaving him anonymous. Additionally, he might take someone else out just to keep the cops busy and confused.

By the time he arrived at the hotel it was midnight. He went directly to his room and settled in for the night. Tomorrow was another day, and it will be a day for planning and strategizing.

In the morning Brack woke up with an interesting idea. What if his next hit was on a cop? Cops were usually "hands off" because of the emotional drama they create within a police department. But they would also be a great distraction and might even reduce the effort placed on guarding Kate. He had to study out the option of a hit on a cop. But first he was going to go to the hospital and pay a visit to Kate's room. He had to see if there was an outside window to her room, and if there was, would there be a way of targeting the room from another building? He also wanted to see what kind of security they had placed on her. He had to decide if it would be better to come at her from inside the hospital, or from outside.

He entered the hospital around ten AM, late enough to not seem suspicious, and he walked a few of the halls making sure that no one connected him with just inspecting Kate's room. He found Kate's room on an outside wall, but also saw that there were not any buildings close by and in the vicinity that would give him a clear shot into her room. He also saw two cops seated outside her room, guarding her. This was not going to be easy. He would most likely have to wait till she was leaving the hospital in order for him to complete his assassination mission.

For this particular assignment he liked doing his hits in pairs. It was just another trick to throw off the cops. All the executions had been in pairs except the last one, and that was because he lost the drone, or else he would have also shot someone at random in the parking lot. He was going to do another fake execution, this time two cops. That should create an enormous fuss if he did a pair of them.

He drove to the Helena Police Department on the northwest corner of Fuller Avenue and Lawrence Street. On the opposite side of the street, on the southwest corner, was the perfect building with a flat roof where he could easily position himself. On this roof he had clear shots at officers walking in and out of the building. There was some kind of street festival going on in the northern section of Fuller Avenue which would cause the perfect diversion. And there was a perfect escape route to the south across several buildings. He could not have found a better place for this hit. But then he had a thought, *would it not be more fun to hit the FBI office. Wouldn't that create an even bigger fuss*?

He decided to scope out the FBI offices on West 15th Street, which were close. He went there but found this more challenging. There was the perfect parking garage building across the street where he could hide and set his target, but the problem was, how does he tell an FBI agent apart from any of the other Federal employees that worked in the same building? They all looked and dressed the same. Eventually he gave up the idea of an FBI hit and decided that the hit would have to be on the local police station, and tomorrow would be the day.

He woke up early, excited that he had a plan. He knew what he was going to do and he was excited to move forward. He left early, about five AM, so he could get to the site and get on the roof before anyone spotted him. He found a fire escape that, with a little manipulation he was able to scale to the top. Along the way he had found a perfect place to hide the rifle, in a roof vent. He would leave the rifle there for a couple of days after the shooting and then retrieve it. That was a necessary move in case anyone saw him, he did not want to be carrying the rifle.

Once on the roof he made his way to the northeast corner of the building, laid down on his stomach which was his favorite shooting position because it gave him the most stability, and waited. And he waited.

The wait was not too long. About 6:30 AM people started moving in and out of the police station. He could not identify who the detectives were because they weren't wearing uniforms, so he would have to hit a couple of street cops, just because they were visible and wearing uniforms.

He waited. At about 6:45 he saw a pair of cops, each in their uniforms, a male and a female, which had conveniently made themselves easy targets. They seemed to be in deep conversation, and the girl giggled occasionally. Brack could not tell if they were in a relationship, like marriage or just boyfriend-girlfriend, or if they were just flirting and the guy was hot to get into her pants. Whatever it was, they seemed to enjoy each other's company and, as far as Brack was concerned, they made easy targets. His evil streak hoped that the guy was married to someone else and that his wife would always wonder why the two had been killed together. Maybe she would assume some jealous boyfriend or husband of the girl decided to take revenge. Brack hoped that his assassination would have a bigger effect than just riling up the police.

Brack aimed carefully, and then in quick succession fired once, and then twice. The cops were laid out on the street, never knowing what hit them. Everyone else in the area scrambled for safety, looking around, unsure where the shots had come from.

The job was finished and Brack scrambled. He hid the rifle, climbed off the roof, making sure no one saw him, quickly made his way to his car, and drove off. Now the waiting game would begin. He would check daily to see if and when Kate would be getting out of the hospital. Whenever it happened, he would make sure he was ready.

THIRTY-TWO

Matthew Christ couldn't leave it alone. He felt he had been wronged. He was convinced he had been wronged, and Jill was the cause. She had ruined his reputation and his good name. And he was not going to stand for it. He was going to confront her and make her confess that she had wronged him. He wanted her to say that he had not done anything to sexually intimidate her. That was all her imagination.

Matthew decided to go to the Helena police station that very day and talk to her. He would make a scene if necessary; whatever it took to discredit her. In his mind he had gone through an exceptional amount of embarrassment because of her, being taken off the lead position for the serial murder case, and then having had her file a sexual misconduct report on his behavior.

He arrived at the police station early that morning, and just as he was about to enter police office, he heard two shots ring out. He immediately recognized the sound as a hunting rifle, and he searched around to see where the shots were coming from. The shots had stopped and he charged over to side of the two downed police officers, finding them both having mortal wounds through the chest. The bullets had been large in caliber and their deaths had been instantaneous, the bullet having gone completely through them and leaving big holes on the opposite sides of their bodies. There was nothing left to do which would help them.

In the adrenaline rush, Matthew had not realized that one of the bullets must have ricocheted off somewhere along the line and had hit him in the lower portion of the left leg. He suddenly felt the sharp pain in his leg and fell to the ground. By now there were a half dozen police officers that came rushing out of the office and seeing to the three wounded individuals. There was not any more that could be done for the two street cops, but for the FBI agent, an ambulance was ordered, and was quick to arrive.

Matthew was rushed off to the hospital and after he was stitched up, he found himself in the room next door to Kate. The reason for having their room in close proximity was so the guards could keep an eye on both rooms just in case Matthew was indeed a target as well.

All the news channels were filled with the story. "Two cops killed in broad daylight and an FBI agent injured. Was this the work of the drone suicide bomber who had lost his drone? Was he still striking more individuals? One hero cop from the FBI was also shot. Is the drone killer trying to reduce the number of people looking for him?" The news stories went on and on for hours filled with speculation and meaningless banter.

Matthew was labelled a hero by all the news sources. His story was told that, "In spite of his personal risk he charged out in the midst of danger to check on and help his fellow officers."

That changed everything. Matthew's entire perspective changed in the blink of an eye. Now that he was a hero, confronting Jill was out of the question. Even though he hated her at this point, confronting her could only add embarrassment and ridicule. So, Matthew decided to bask in his glory.

He was released after only one day in the hospital. His leg had been adequately stitched up and, although he limped, he was able to get around with crutches. He left without a police escort, being convinced that the attack was not intended for him.

In the meantime, as can be expected, the Police and the FBI were in an uproar. An emergency meeting was called in the police conference room on the afternoon of the shooting. Conrad started the meeting by asking for a moment of silence in memory of the fallen police officers. Then he turned to Matthew who was on the view screen and was asked to present his version of the shooting. Matthew explained, "I was just going to visit the police station and talk to Conrad about the progress of the investigation since we had the shooting of the second individual connected with the base. I was walking next to the two patrol cops that were shot and happened to catch one of the bullets that had gone clean through one of them. I was not the target and I have no idea what would have made them a target, other than that this was another one of those random killings performed by the drone killer. He has some kind of grudge against the police."

Then one of the local detectives explained, "I was one of the first on the scene, coming out of the building immediately after the shooting and I tried to figure out where the shots had come from. I asked the people in the area if they had seen a shooter or if they had heard directions for the shot being fired. They said that they heard something in the direction of the shopping mall across Lawrence Street but could not see anything specific. I saw that the officers were beyond help so I ran over to the building. There were four cars parked on the side of the street and I looked in each of them but they were all empty. I looked into the shop windows, but there was nothing there either. My next thought was the roof so I climbed to the top of the building and went to the northern edge of the roof, but again nothing."

The CSI lead jumped in, "The shots were fired in a downward trajectory, and the trajectory came from the roof so we went up there as well and did a thorough search but found nothing. This guy is obviously a professional and knows how to cover his tracks. We also collected whatever surveillance videos we could find, but so far, we have not found anything specific. However. we are not done looking. We still have a lot that we need to go through."

Conrad spoke up, "This guy is definitely really good. Do you see what he has done? He is distracted us and threw both of our departments into complete turmoil. All of a sudden, all our resource efforts have shifted from finding this drone killer to searching for a cop killer. I am not saying that we shouldn't have shifted our focus, but it makes me feel like we're starting all over, with a new set of weapons, and a new area of search. This guy is making me angry and I hope I am never in an interview room alone with him because I might end up breaking a few police protocols."

"Amen to that," commented the Chief of Police.

"So, what do we do?" Conrad asked the group. "You are telling me that there is no evidence of anything related to this killer. The CSI team has found nothing. The witnesses on the scene saw nothing. Yet we have two dead cops and an injured FBI agent. So, what do we do?"

Jill spoke up and said, "We have pictures of all the vehicles that were in the area. We are going to visit and interview each of the owners of these vehicles. We are also going out to interview all the shops in the area. We are not going to leave any stone unturned. Somebody has to know something. Somebody has to have seen something. We are flipping over every stone over until we have something to work on."

Conrad continued, "Excellent. And we still have the team going through the videos. Other than that, I want everyone to refocus on the work that you were doing before these most recent shootings. We were making excellent progress and that we're more likely to find this guy through the areas we were already working on, since the latest shooting doesn't seem to yield much. I just want this bugger caught and I want to put an end to any more killings."

Jill added, "Unfortunately we are assuming it's the same guy. It is, but someone should check into the background of our two dead officers to see if in fact there would have been a reason to expect a new shooter who is hiding under the guise of the drone assassin. I will put a couple of my homicide detectives on that. However, let me stress, that I personally believe it is the same guy, but we need to make sure. We cannot screw this up."

There was a silent pause in the meeting and then Conrad added, "If there are no other comments related to the finding of this assassin, then I am going to call an end to this meeting so we can all get back to work. More silence so Conrad ended the meeting.

THIRTY-THREE

It had been a couple days since the shooting of the police officers, and Brack was still on the loose. The police were no closer to finding him than before. Brack visited the hospital several times a day, hoping to zero in on Kate's departure. He did not want to ask specifically about her because he was sure that the police had warned everyone in the hospital to be on the lookout for anyone asking questions about Kate. He also avoided walking directly by her room. He wasn't sure if there was a camera planted on that location and he didn't want to be recognized by the officers guarding the room as someone who comes by regularly. He did not want to raise suspicions.

He knew it would be a random lucky break if he happened to be in the right place at the right time to see her departure. He would stake out the departure doors of the hospital in the afternoon, realizing that most hospital releases were in the afternoon after the doctor had given the patient a release. He hoped that she would be returning to the same hotel, the Holiday Inn Express, but he was not sure. His back-up plan was that if he missed her leaving the hospital, he would watch the hotel, and if that did not work, he would watch the entrance to the base. One way or another he would catch her and finish the job.

After the third day since the shooting, he snuck back on the roof of the strip mall and retrieved his hunting rifle. He was thrilled to find it was undisturbed. The police obviously had not made the connection that the roof was where he had positioned himself for the shootings.

Now that he had his rifle back, he was ready to take out Kate. He could find a good location at the hotel or near the military base and then he would easily be able to finish the job.

In the meantime, Kate had been in contact with Dick whose first comment was, "I heard about you on the news and went up to visit you but they would not let me into the hospital room to see you. Apparently, I wasn't on some approved list of visitors. How are you doing anyway?"

"I'm doing okay and should be out of here in a day or two, just in time to see you guys play," responded Kate. "But I will not be up to doing a lot of dancing just yet. Maybe by the following weekend. We will have to see how it goes."

"Hope to see you Saturday," responded Dick. "We missed your support the last couple times. We look forward to you being our groupie once again."

"Sounds fun," replied Kate.

A short time later her boss, Dereck Hardness, arrived at her room and asked, "How are you doing?"

"Anxious to get back at it," was Kate's response. "I don't want all my work up to this point to go stale."

"I'm with you on that," responded Dereck. "Unfortunately, I am going to have to leave Helena. I have another project that is struggling and I need to give them some support. I have confidence that you will be back at it here in a few days and that you'll be able to wrap up your work soon enough."

"I agree," responded Kate. "I will get this wrapped up soon enough. Hope you have a good trip and that you get that other project back on track."

"I'm not worried," responded Dereck. "I'll stay in touch in case you have any additional problems here."

With that Dereck departed for the airport.

Kate also had some additional interviews with the police, each time hoping that some new information would come out of the conversation but nothing new ever came up.

It was exactly two days later when Kate was finally given permission to leave the hospital, and she was instructed to maintain bedrest for at least another week. But no one really thought that would happen. Kate was too much of a fireball to just sit around for seven more days. She felt weak, but antsy, and after a day the antsyness won out. She contacted the commander and the VC on the base and informed them that she would be back the following day to continue her work.

The local police maintained their protective detail, keeping close to Kate. The contract that had been placed on her was still active and, now that two cops had been killed, the police were convinced the drone serial killer was still active. They were convinced the primary reason he was still in Helena and had staged another distractive killing was to finish his assassination of Kate. Hence, watching Kate would be critical for her personal protection, but it may also be the best way to lure out the killer.

The police guard was placed outside of Kate's hotel room door, which made the other guests nervous, but there was no other way to manage the situation. A second police guard was placed in thc lobby, and he monitored everyone that went into and out of the hotel. The two guards would switch off every couple hours, just for the sake of variety.

The following morning Kate got up early and got ready to head to the base. She was still on heavy pain drugs, which gave her a false sense of security, but she was smart enough to know that she was not able to do anything strenuous. She did not want to be cut open again in order to fix something she had torn or damaged. She knew the importance of the healing process, and she would take every precaution, but having been bed bound for several days had driven her crazy. She wanted to get her mind working again.

The police escort came with her as far as the gates of the base, at which point a military guard took over the task of keeping her safe. Two military police replaced the local police in her vehicle, and they drove to the commander's office. Once at the office she was immediately escorted into the office where the commander and the VC were waiting for her. The commander spoke first saying, "Welcome back. I cannot believe you're back already after having been shot three times. How are you doing?" He sincerely sounded concerned, which surprised Kate.

"I'm extremely sore," responded Kate, "but I'm also drugged into oblivion so I'm feeling okay for now. I just did not want to lose traction on my work here in finding the mole so I insisted on coming back and continuing my work."

"We're glad you're back and able to get around, even if it's slowly," responded the VC. "Give us an update on where you're at and what you expect to do next."

Kate explained, "I have the mole list narrowed down to about twenty individuals, and I have interviewed most of them. I have been monitoring their communications and I've been looking for anything suspicious. However, I am now convinced that they are not communicating through normal channels, because I am not spotting any anomalies. I actually expected that but I needed to be thorough, so I went through the work of reviewing all the normal channels of communication. What I need to do next is lock in on all non-official communications channels, like personal cell phones."

"I'm still convinced that this mole hunt is a complete waste of time," complained the commander. "I'd still prefer we put a stop to this and quit invading everyone's personal privacy."

"Unfortunately, mole hunts are all about invading personal privacy because that's usually how treasonous data is transmitted," explained Kate. "You'd be surprised how much we learn during one of these mole hunts, most of which is never revealed because it's irrelevant to the mission."

"These are all glowing and wonderful statements, but I believe it's all bull," barked the commander. He became agitated by the entire inquiry. "If you find one piece of personal information on anyone in this command, that you think should not be made public, I'll give you free reign on your investigation. I challenge you to come back to me by the end of the day with some revealing insights that would surprise me. If you do, you have free reign, and if you do not, I'd like to see you call this off and leave."

Kate was irritated and decided to do a little disclosure, "I do not need to wait till the end of the day. I can do that right now. You are so arrogant and self-righteous that you think you are immune to investigation, but I already have enough dirt on your organization to make it stink like cow manure. So, you are on. If I disclose anything to you right now that you would not want to be made public, then you'll quit hassling me and let me do my job, correct?"

"Correct, you little twirp. Let us hear what you've got."

Kate was ready, "I would like to show you a video of Commander Planter and VC Forengi entering a hotel together for a rendezvous and included in that video are some explicit pictures of what went on during that meeting. Since you aggressively and arrogantly pushed me, I will give you the choice. Do I send a copy of the video to you, or to the media?"

The commander was speechless, and he stared at the VC, not knowing how to respond. Then he turned to Kate and said, "You SOB!"

The VC turned to the commander and angrily blurted out, "You dumb jackass. I told you we needed to be more careful. You were in such a hurry to get into my pants that your brain quit working. Now you may possibly have destroyed both of our careers."

Kate kept quiet. She knew she had won this one and by saying anything at this point she would simply increase everyone's level of anger. She sat and waited.

The commander was silent for a good ten minutes. He knew this could not only destroy his family, but if he ended up divorced, it would put a black mark on his military record which would affect his entire career. Someone in his position was supposed to be above reproach. He felt devastated.

Finally, the commander spoke up, "You win. I will stay out of your investigation and let you have free reign. And I hope I never have to meet with you or see you again!"

"That doesn't work for me," corrected Kate. "I will need to do report-outs with you and with your VC. But at this point I can no longer trust either of you to give me the type of support I need in order to continue this investigation. So, I need someone with command authority to work with me and get me the information and the clearances I need in order to finish my job. None of what I am demanding is optional. Who do you want me to work with?"

The commander barked, "Conner Brighton, the Base Operations Commander, would be the next in charge and he can give you the support you need."

This was almost the last thing Kate wanted to hear. She remembered Conner Brighton as a chauvinistic pig who had made sexist remarks to her during her earlier interview with him. She dreaded the idea that she was going to have to work with him on this project.

"I want you to call him and have him come to the office right now so you can tell him that he has to give me one hundred percent cooperation," demanded Kate, who was now fully in control of the situation. She was going to make this work if it kills her.

"Okay," said the commander, feeling fully defeated, as he dialed the phone. He instructed Conner to urgently rush to his office which fortunately was close. The Base Operations Commander arrived at the office about ten minutes later as the three sat in silence waiting.

Once Conner arrived, Commander Planter instructed him, "The Pentagon has given strict orders for Kate here, which I know you have already met, to do a mole hunt on the base here, and you have been designated to be her confidential and complete support person on the base. I am not sure what she will need, but this is a Pentagon priority, so we need to give our full cooperation."

Conner looked at the commander and said, "I thought you were against this mole hunt."

"I've been overridden in a big way," responded the commander. "This is the way it has to be."

"I'll do whatever I need to do," responded Conner.

"Thanks," responded the commander. Then he turned to Kate and asked, "Are we through here?"

"Yes," responded Kate. Then turning to Conner she said, "I need to go with you to your office right now so we can discuss next steps."

"Definitely," said a cooperative Conner. The two left the office and as they were walking away, they could hear the VC screaming at the commander, calling him names that would make a sailor blush. Conner commented, "You obviously got a rise out of those two. I am not sure what went on in there, and I do not want to know either, but I get the impression we're talking about something pretty serious here."

"That we are," commented Kate. "That we are."

As they walked along Conner continued, "Previously when we met, I was on a wavelength that wanted you out of my office as quickly as possible and I may have said a few things that were unbecoming, and I now need to apologize for those comments. I am not the sexist pig that you may believe me to be. I was just trying to get rid of you. You will see a different side of me from now on."

"I'm relieved to hear all that," responded Kate. "When they mentioned that I would be working with you I was not very excited. But now that you have explained your position, I feel we can probably work well together."

"My opinion exactly."

THIRTY-FOUR

Conner had a mild mannered and friendly personality. His six-foot stance, and his muscular build, made him stand out as someone that you do not mess with, and his open and sharing personality did not support that perception. There was also a very sincere side to him which made him helpful to the members of his unit. He would go out of his way to spend time comforting the people around him when they needed a listening ear. And he was very good at and sincerely made them feel better.

Conner followed the lead of most men in command position on the base in that he had no facial hair and had his head shaved. He wore his uniform day and night and some of the people in his command joked that he probably also slept in his uniform. But in spite of his "all business" demeanor, he was a family man with a wife and four kids at home and they enjoyed spending time with him. They looked forward to their Sunday wrestling matches with their dad, and occasionally he would even let them win.

Kate walked with Conner Brighton, the Base Operations Commander, to his office in the command building. They walked in silence. They entered his office, shut the door, sat down on opposite sides of his desk, and he asked, "So tell me what's going on here and what it is that I'm supposed to be doing?"

Kate went through a review of everything she had done up to this point, focusing on the text messages that were sent out and noting that it was someone in the command of the base that had to be the mole based on messages they picked up using foreign intelligence services. She explained the interviews that she had performed, and the results that she had received from those interviews. She explained, "The most positive evidence that we have, which convinces us that we have a conspiracy here, is the fact that Commander Mark Simeon was shot and killed. I have also been shot three times and that I was obviously supposed to have been killed in the process. The drone hits that were on private citizens were obviously intended to throw the police off track, including the recent murders of the two police officers. The real purpose of all the attacks was to get us off the mole hunt. It is too big a coincidence the two individuals who were the most focused on this investigation were both shot."

"You're scaring me a little," responded the Base Operations Commander. "Now that I'm the lead on the base side, does that make me a target?"

"I have no answer to that," responded Kate, "but you can see the seriousness of what we've been tasked to do here."

"Definitely," responded Conner. "So, what are your next steps?"

"We need to set another trap," commented Kate. "I am not sure what form that trap should take, but we need to narrow down our search. One thing I want to do and that I need your help with is that I want to send out another false message. Another thing I need to do, since I have not had any luck reviewing the communications that have occurred through normal channels, is that I need to tap into the various personal phones of the individuals who are in the command so I can get a history of their communications. Somehow these communications are occurring, but I still do not have a handle on that. Is there a way for you to get me all the personal cell numbers of all the command leadership, along with their personal email addresses? I assume you do not need a subpoena since this is the military and you have different rules here."

"I'll figure out a way to help you with both of those items," responded Conner. "But you realize that they may have a second phone that they use for these mole communications, and you may not find anything by searching their personal phones."

"Understood," responded Kate. "But I would hate to miss something that should have been obvious. These criminals are not as smart as we give them credit for."

"Tell me what you want me to do in this false message?" asked Conner.

"I need you to communicate a message in a time phased manner," responded Kate. "The last mole hunt message that we sent out took about two days before the message was discovered in North Korea. So, this time I want to send out the false message to two individuals, then wait a day, then another two individuals, then wait a day, and so on. My hope is that based on the timing of when the message is received at the other end it will help me narrow down who I am looking for."

"Understood," responded Conner. "I will start on that today by creating a message and giving it to the first two individuals. I will also get you the cell and email information for the individuals in the command and I have a techie who you can work directly and secretively to help you get access to and to search these communications channels. I have someone who is really good and is not on your top twenty list so he should be trustable. Would that be helpful?"

"That would be perfect," responded Kate. "When can I start working with this techie of yours?"

"Actually, I'll introduce the two of you right now," responded Conner as he dialed the phone and requested the techie to come to his office.

After brief introductions, Conner said, "Bilco, I need you to work with Kate here on a top-secret assignment. I cannot have anyone know anything about what you are doing here. This is a mole hunt that has been ordered by the Pentagon." Then turning to Kate he said, "Bilco has his own private office where the two of you can camp out for the next few days as you work on this assignment."

Bilco spoke up next and asked, "What is it you will need me to do?"

Kate responded, "I need to look at the correspondence of several individuals. I need to look into their personal emails and phone conversations. I need to be able to search through them and see if there is anything suspicious."

"Wow," responded Bilco. "That is personal. Is that even legal?"

Conner responded, "When they joined the military, they signed a document that gives us permission to investigate their personal lives, and this falls under that approval."

"Okay," said Bilco. "I just don't want to get into trouble here."

Conner responded, "You are doing this under the Pentagon's, the commander's and my direction and command. If there is any kickback, the buck stops here."

"This must really be a big deal," responded Bilco.

"That it is," responded Conner.

Then Kate asked, "When can we start working on this?"

"I'll start looking into it today," responded Bilco. "If you can join me in the morning, I should already have some stuff for you to look at."

"Perfect," said Kate. "I'll join you in your office in the morning."

At this point Kate was feeling pretty drained anyway, and she decided to make her way back to the hotel. She informed the local police that she would be leaving the base and they came to the gate of the base, ready to escort her back to her hotel.

The drive back to the hotel was without incident, for which everyone was thankful. Once in her room, Kate crashed immediately and was asleep, almost before she got undressed.

The following morning Kate was anxious to return to the base and find out what Bilco had researched. She got up, got ready, and had the police escort her to the base, where the military police again resumed her escort and brought her to Bilco's office. Once there she asked, "What did you find?"

Bilco responded, "I have started downloading phone conversations for the past month for several of the command individuals that you are interested in. I have the information ready for you on a computer terminal over on my backup desk and you can start reviewing them whenever you are ready."

"Incredible," responded Kate. Bilco showed her where the download files were located and how she could identify each of the individuals that had made the correspondence. Within minutes she was studying the correspondence, looking for cryptic or coded messages and trying to make sense of what she was seeing. It was a long, hard, and tedious task, reading every message and trying to determine if it could have hidden meaning. But she was in her element, searching for a mole, and she was thrilled to have the support she needed to further this investigation along.

Kate and Bilco spent the entire day searching through the transcripts and had only made it through about one-third of the command staff, but they felt successful having gotten as far as they had. Another couple days and they will have everyone successfully reviewed. They were anxious and excited about the progress they had made.

In the early afternoon, two of Conner's staff entered the room where Bilco and Kate were working, and the one individual, Mireille, who was responsible for the base's housing, asked, "What are you guys working on? I need my support structure analysis and you seem to be delaying that for some reason? And why is a civilian in here with all the security information at her disposal?"

Titus, from the facilities maintenance command, the other individual who had entered the room, asked, "What is she working on?"

Bilco was slightly taken aback and responded, "You do not usually get that report for another few days. Why is it so important all of a sudden? I am not sure you ever look at it anyway. And as far as Kate working here, you will have to ask Commander Conner about that because he authorized her to be here."

"I'll do exactly that," barked Mireille as she stomped out of the room and slammed the door behind her.

Near the end of the day, Conner came to Kate and reported, "We sent out a message through two individuals yesterday, and we sent out a slightly different message through two more individuals today. At this point I have nothing to report as far as a message coming through at the other end."

"Thanks for the update," responded Kate. "We should be able to wrap this up in the next few days. Even though we have not found anything yet, we are making excellent progress."

"Good to hear," responded Conner. "Let me know if you need anything."

Bilco spoke up, "Mireille was in here today, making a fuss about a report that she usually does not receive for another few days. She and Titus were questioning why Kate is in here. They were challenging what she was doing in here and I told her to talk to you."

"Interesting because they never came to me," responded Conner. "I wonder what that was about."

"They're nosey and busy-bodies," responded Bilco. "They know something is up and they can't handle not knowing everything that's going on."

The day was done and there would not be any work on the mole hunt over the weekend. Bilco had plans which took him away to family for the next couple of days so Kate decided she would pay more attention to her recovery during that time. She returned to the hotel with the usual escorts, and settled in for the weekend, but first she was going to go out playing groupie to her new favorite cowboy band. Since it was Friday, it meant a drive to Butte, but that was just an hour away and in Montana that is considered to be down the street.

Kate went to Butte with her police escort and joined them at the band's table, close to the stage. She would not be dancing, and the band members all knew that she would just be sitting it out with them and enjoying the music. She felt like she was one of the group, just there to have fun. Dick spent as much time with her as possible, and the two had an enjoyable night. Kate ended up leaving a little early because she was becoming tired and a little groggy from the pain meds. She did not want to have any trouble during the drive home.

The next day, Saturday evening she spent almost entirely in her room. She had overdone it the previous day, spending the day at the base and the evening in Butte listening to the cowboy band. She hurt more than usual, even with the pain meds. So, she spent the day watching meaningless garbage on the television. She hated the news because it was nothing but opinions and did not actually give any news, and the sports this time of year were dull because it was between football seasons. So, she flipped through the channels a couple times and finding nothing else to watch she bored herself to tears with old movies.

That afternoon she made a few phone calls. One was to her boss, giving him an update of her progress at the base. She told him about the threats she had to make in order to get the commander to comply, causing her boss to laugh and say, "That sounds like my Kate!" He had requested that she keep him informed just in case there were any complications with her injuries. Additionally, he was concerned about the contract that was still out on her and he wanted to make sure he could finish her job if for any reason she was completely incapacitated.

Kate also told him about Dick, and the fact she had been going out to be a band groupie on Friday and Saturday nights. She found it important to be an open book with her boss, because he had always stressed that even the smallest detail could become critical. And there have been times in the past where this was exactly the case. Sometimes it is the details that make the difference in an investigation's success or failure.

Another call she made was to a contact that she had in the CIA. This was someone she had worked with on a previous project, and she had maintained the relationship just-in-case she might need the contact in the future. Her current investigation turned out to be just such a situation where she needed CIA help. The CIA agent asked, "How's it going with the mole hunt?"

Kate responded, "It is going fine. I will probably have it nailed down within the next few days."

The CIA agent responded with the comment, "Back off. Slow down the process a little. We do not want this mole to be exposed too quickly. We need him to keep being a mole for another week or so. I have a special message I want you to send out. I will text it to you so you have the exact wording."

"Okay," responded Kate. "It was all very mysterious."

Then the CIA agent said, "Don't forget who you're really working for!"

Saturday, she went to the club to listen to the cowboy band. She almost felt obligated to go there since she had attended Friday, which had been a much longer drive. But in the end, she enjoyed the music and the conversation, so she returned to her hotel that evening invigorated and renewed.

Sunday was not much better than Saturday. Another boring day. Tomorrow would be Monday, and a chance to get back to her search for the mole.

THIRTY-FIVE

Brack Hellringer was starting to get a little frustrated. First, he missed Kate's departure from the hospital. He was there most of the day, but he ended up waiting at the wrong hospital exit and her police escort took her out of a back door that Brack was not monitoring. Unknowingly he ended up waiting in that lobby for an extra day and a half after she had already departed. He only realized she had departed when he walked past the hallway where her room had been and found that there were no longer any guards posted there.

Brack correctly assumed that she would be going back to the same hotel. He thought she was a little smarter than that, and that she would mix it up a bit, going to a different hotel just to throw him off. Lucky for him she had gone back to the same hotel. When he was checking out of the hotel he walked in through the lobby, acting as if he belonged there, and he noticed the police guard sitting in the lobby. That told him right away that he had found her hotel. Then he went up to the second floor and found a guard at one of the doors halfway down the hall. He continued up the stairway to the third floor, acting again like he belonged there. He had found his target. Now what he needed to do was to stake out the hotel and watch for a golden opportunity to finish his assignment.

He missed her the first day. He knew he had missed her because when he arrived at the hotel, the lobby guard was gone. He went to the base around the time he was expecting her to depart, and again he had missed her because she had left early. He was becoming frustrated. He started cursing, asking why someone was stopping him from completing his assignment.

The next day he arrived at her hotel early, checked to see the guard in the lobby, and camped out in his rental car in the parking lot. He waited for about one hour and then the three of them, Kate and her two guards, exited the hotel. One guard rode with Kate in her car, and the other followed them in a police cruiser. They drove through Starbucks so Kate could get her Green Tea Frappuccino with no sweetener and six scoops of the maccha powder, and then headed directly to the base. At the base, the police officer that was riding with Kate transferred to the police cruiser, and they departed. The police were replaced by base security forces who did the same thing, one riding in Kate's car and a second officer following them in a patrol car. At this point Brack lost control of Kate's movements.

Brack waited outside the base for hours, waiting for Kate to depart the base once again. Eventually she did but, to his frustration, the police escort also arrived as she was departing and they took over their role of escorting her back to her hotel. Then the waiting game started again. Brack gave up around six PM, missing the drive that Kate and her escorts made to Butte. He did not expect to see her again that day.

The following day was Saturday. Brack watched to see any of Kate's movements, but nothing happened. She had followed the instructions of her police guards and ordered fast food delivered to her hotel room, including pizza in the evening. Brack once again gave up his surveillance too early and missed Kate's departure to the country western bar. Brack was starting to resign himself to the fact that maybe assassinating Kate would also require the execution of another cop or two.

Sunday was not any better for Brack. Then it finally was Monday, Kate followed the same routine as before. Brack followed her and her escorts, hoping to find that golden opportunity where he could make his hit. In the end, he decided the best opportunity would again be in the parking lot of the hotel. There were not any buildings around that he could use as cover. He felt that his best position would be the roof of the Buffalo Wild Wings restaurant. Unfortunately, that was a risky location, with only one option for getting on and off the roof. A better option might be to just do it as a drive-by shooting, but he knew that his car and his face would be captured on video. If he did that option, he would have to steal a car, use a ski mask, and wear gloves.

After working it through his mind several times, he decided on the drive-by option. He would hit the police officers first, since they had weapons, then he would shoot Kate. That was the only thing that seemed like it would work. He had formulated his plan, and now it was time for execution.

The following morning, he stole a car from the mall parking lot just west of the Holiday Inn. He assumed that the cars in the parking lot were most likely employees who wouldn't miss the car for at least four hours or more. Since the employee cars were at the far end of the parking lot, he assumed that the surveillance cameras would not be able to record very much detail. He also assumed that, if he did the switch quick enough, the cops would probably not even make the connection with the attempt on Kate's life.

He had left his car in the same area, ready to be switched back into as soon as the shooting was finished. Then he drove to the hotel parking lot bright and early. He parked in such a way that he had a clear view of the front entrance of the hotel, which is where Kate normally exited and entered the hotel. Then he waited.

Eventually Kate and her two police escorts exited the hotel, the cops leading the way. The police were on either side of Kate and slightly in front of her. They obviously took their job seriously, they stopped for a moment, scanning the parking lot for any obvious signs of an attacker. That turned out to be their mistake. Somehow, they missed seeing Brack.

Their exit was Brack's trigger. He rolled down the windows on the passenger's side of the vehicle, pulled down the ski mask over his head, and raced through the breezeway in the front of the hotel and barely in front of the officers. The officers attempted to pull out their weapons, realizing that this was an attack, but they were too slow. Brack stopped abruptly in front of the cops and, using his pistol, he fired two shots at each of the police officers. Then, as they were falling out of his way, he emptied his pistol out on Kate. He watched her fall, almost as if it was in slow motion. Then he sped off, exiting the parking lot and driving around the outside of the mall to the location where he had stolen the car. He pulled off his ski mask and quickly switched vehicles, getting back into his own rental car. Then he drove off, heading back to his own hotel where he returned to his room and decided it was time for him to take a nap. He was tired, having gotten up earlier than normal. He was confident that this time he had completed his task. All he could say, as he entered his room and got ready to take a nap, was, "Sixty, sixty-one, and sixty-two. This time I am sure I can count Kate." This time he had made a mistake.

Emergency vehicles arrived within ten minutes, having been called by the hotel staff. There were a couple of ambulances, fire engines, and about ten police cruisers, all jammed into the front end of the Holiday Inn Express Hotel. Outside of them was a ring of news vans, hot to get a story on the latest murders that they were all sure was connected to the drone killer. The news was not good. Both cops had received two shots, one in the chest and one in the head, the assassin's favorite pattern for executions. They were both dead before they hit the ground. It was obviously a professional hit by someone who knew how to kill.

Kate was barely still alive, having received four bullets this time. The EMTs debated whether they should call for a helicopter, but in the end, they decided that an ambulance could get her to the hospital quicker so they loaded her up and raced off with her, proceeded by two police cruisers as an escort.

At the hospital, the emergency services people were desperate to try to save Kate. She had become the symbol of success in conquering the drone assassin. But this time her injuries looked desperately serious. One shot had grazed the side of her head, which was most likely the shot that had left her unconscious. A second shot had hit her in the chest, dead center on her right nipple, which was probably the shot intended for her heart, but which had been off slightly, just like the shot to the head had been off. This second bullet had gone clean through her body.

A third bullet hit her on the right-hand side of her stomach, which was possibly the shot that could eventually kill her. She must have turned slightly sideways because all the shots were slightly off and this one went diagonally across her internal organs. There was so much damage to many of her vital organs that her survival was questionable. The fourth shot hit the side of her right arm and broke her bone, then continued into her side, ending up in her right lung.

Kate went immediately into surgery, with two teams working on her, one focused on her upper body and the second on her abdomen. Both teams were fearful about her eventual survival. The surgeries were completed, as best they possibly could, realizing that a potential organ transplant would eventually become necessary for her liver and kidney and possibly also her lung. It did not look good. For now, her recovery time in the hospital would take several weeks, and her primary doctor, Brenda Kidman, who was the same doctor that had worked on her earlier, worried that she may never regain consciousness. Even with a CT scan to her head, they could not predict how serious the damage to her brain had been.

The medical authorities immediately notified her boss Dereck Hardness because he had been there during her previous injuries, and they knew that he would be able to notify any next of kin that may exist. Dereck, of course, was in shock. At first, he was angry that the police escort was ineffective, but then when he learned that the two officers had also been killed, he suddenly felt sorry for them, having given their lives in their attempt to keep Kate safe. He made immediate plans to return to Kate's bedside. He knew that at this point he would need to assume the completion of Kate's assignment.

Brack flipped on the news in order to see what the report was on his hit. He chuckled when he saw the police arresting the owner of the car that he had stolen, but he knew that they would quickly figure out that he had nothing to do with the crime. Then he went ballistic, throwing stuff around in his hotel room. He just learned that only two people had been killed and that Kate was still alive with little chance of survival. He had convinced himself that he had finished her off this time, but apparently four bullets weren't enough.

After Brack calmed down, he thought about his situation and he decided that he was not going to leave Helena until he knew for sure that Kate was dead, even if that took a month. He was not leaving again, just to have to return one more time to Montana. This time he would wait it out. If there was any chance of her coming out of that hospital, he was going to be there waiting for her. But first she would have to regain consciousness, and right now that seemed doubtful.

THIRTY-SIX

Dereck Hardness arrived in Helena and went directly to the hospital in order to check on Kate. He found her in the ICU hooked up to all sorts of monitors and life sustaining equipment. He could hardly tell it was her because of all the medical equipment she was attached to and bandaging. She was a frightful sight to behold.

He had a conversation with the staff and asked, "How's she doing and what's her prognosis?"

They were blunt and honest, "Not good. She has had severe damage to several organs and we are not sure if she will ever come out of her coma. The hit to her head was pretty hard causing a fracture." Then they asked about an Advanced Medical Directive for her in case she is deemed unrecoverable.

Dereck informed them that she did not have any family that he knew of and that he had been the only family she had ever known. He explained how she did not even know who her parents were and she had been brought up in the foster care system. The decision on whether to pull the plug on her would need to be made by the doctors.

This left the hospital staff in a quandary. They wanted someone else to have the responsibility of deciding if she should be cut off of life support. They did not want to have that responsibility.

Dereck, seeing that he was of no use at the hospital and that there was nothing he could do to help, decided to leave the hospital and drive over to the base. Along the way he received a call from Jill, the lead homicide detective for Helena, and she stated, "The guards watching Kate tell me that you are in town, which is important because I need you under guard. There is an obvious connection between the killer and the activities at the base, and you are also connected with those activities, so I want to assign two officers to travel with you and keep you under guard. I realize that did not end up helping Kate, but we still feel the need that any guard is better than no guard."

Dereck responded, "I understand your concern and my saying that it is not necessary will not stop you from doing what you think is right. I am on my way to the base right now and I will let you know when I'm leaving the base so you can have my escorts meet me at the entrance to the base."

"Perfect," responded Jill. "I'll have your escort guards ready."

Once at the base he drove directly to the commander's office and requested a meeting. The commander invited him in and asked, "I heard on the news that Kate has been attacked again. How is she doing?"

Dereck, feeling that the commander's concern was somewhat textbook and insincere, responded, "She's unconscious and on life support. They are concerned if she is going to pull through this time."

Then the commander stated, "I guess this will put an end to the inquiries about the mole! This should put an end to the mole hunt!"

"Not at all," responded Dereck. "I am taking over the investigation. The assignment for an inquiry was not given to Kate, it was given to my organization, and we will do whatever needs to be done to weed out this mole, especially now that we feel confident that there is a connection between the mole and the assassin. I have all the information that Kate has collected, and I will be reading it again." Dereck wanted to kill any resistance from the commander. He knew what Kate had gone through with him and he cut to the chase and said, "Kate left me everything, including the videos of you and the VC, and the threat for compliance remains. The only difference is that the face of the investigation will now be me instead of Kate."

The commander was slightly taken aback. He did not realize that Dereck was informed about Kate's threat, and he quickly realized that he was not going to be able to put an end to this investigation. He commented, "I assume you know she has been working with Conner Brighton, the Base Operations Commander. I will have him come to my office so you can meet him and begin working with him."

"Excellent," responded Dereck. The commander placed the call and a few minutes later Conner Brighton arrived. Introductions were made and then Dereck departed the commander's office and walked with Conner to his office, where they sat down and discussed what Kate had been working on and the progress they had made.

"Can you give me an update on anything that's happened in the last couple days while Kate's been out of commission?" asked Dereck.

"Sure," responded Conner. "She has been successful in setting up traps. The one she set up where we time phased a message out to two people at a time has been very successful. So far, we have given the message out to six people and we already know the message has gotten through to the North Koreans. That immediately narrows our list down to these six, but I would suspect that the last two would not have had enough time to send the message, so I would focus on these four individuals. One of them is the mole. I am certain of it. She had me give a slight variation to the messages each time they were sent out, but the way the message was received, the variations did not come through so I cannot narrow it down to only two. We have four, and maybe six, individuals that we'll have to investigate further."

"Excellent," responded Dereck. "As long as one of these four didn't share the message with anyone else and we end up with the message being relayed by a third person."

"We made a big deal about the secrecy of the message and hopefully everyone stuck to that plan, but of course, that's always a possibility," responded Conner. Then he asked, "What do we do next?"

"We need to set up interviews with these four and, without telling them that this is a mole hunt, find out in detail what they've been doing for the last few days," responded Dereck.

"I'll get right on it," answered Conner. "I'm personally anxious to get this over with, not just because we don't want a mole in our presence, but also because this is a major interference to my work schedule."

"Let's do it," responded Dereck. "But let's talk to all six, just in case."

Conner immediately started making phone calls to the six individuals, setting up meetings with each of them throughout the day. He requested that they be ready to answer a few questions about their schedules and activities over the past few days. Then he told Dereck, "Our first interview is in thirty minutes. Does that work for you?"

"Perfect," responded Dereck. "I am going to check to see if they have any electronics on them when they are here. I know that you are researching their military and personal phones, but I am looking for any communications devices that you may not have listed, and I'm going to be cloning them during the interview. Then I can see what communications has occurred using those devices as well."

"Understood," responded Conner. "Let me turn my personal devices off so they don't interfere with the searches you might be doing." He pulled a phone out of his top desk drawer and proceeded to shut it down. He did not realize that Dereck had already cloned that phone as well and was planning to dig through Conner's private correspondence. He was not expecting to find anything, but he also knew better than to ignore any option for discovering this mole.

Then Dereck asked, "Is there somewhere I can sit for the next thirty minutes and make some notes?"

"Of course," responded Conner as he pointed to an office next to his. Then Dereck left Conner's office and settled in next door.

Thirty minutes later, the first interviewee arrived. The meeting was held in Conner's office. He introduced Dereck to the subject being interviewed and then said, "Lieutenant Blanch Taylor, we are trying to dig out an incident that occurred over the last couple of days. It is confidential and we are not going to share any names, but we need to know who might have witnessed or been involved in this incident. Therefore, we need to know your schedule for the last couple of days. Where were you, at what times, and what were your activities? This does not implicate you in any way. What we are actually trying to do is clear you of any involvement. We are looking for an alibi."

"That's a little scary," responded Blanch. "I'll give you whatever you need, but if there was anything that I may have been involved in it would be entirely accidental."

"We're sure of that as well," responded Conner. "Please give us what and where of your activities for the last two days."

With that Blanch listed everything that she was involved in. She told about each of her activities. The interviewers were especially interested in the times when she was alone. Also, as Conner was leading the conversations in the investigation, Dereck was able to scan the area for any additional electronics. He found two private cell phones on Blanch and he proceeded to clone both of them so he could go through her correspondence later that evening when he was in his hotel room. Two private phones put her high on his suspicious list.

The remaining five individuals went through a similar interview process, all of which seemed legitimate. They all were on base and super busy, interacting with their staff. Each had a personal cell phone, but it was the phone that was registered with the base and had already been checked by Conner. Only one other individual, Captain Viola Grant, sounded suspicious because she also had two personal cell phones and because she had spent a considerable part of the day off base in both of the last two days.

Dereck worked with Bilco to get the transcripts of these phones. It took about one hour but soon the transcripts of all the eight phones, the six that were registered and the two that were not, were ready for Dereck's review.

At the end of the day, Dereck took the recordings of the six meetings, along with the telephone transcripts, and left the base, heading for his hotel where he would spend several hours going through the phone transcripts. He called Jill so that she could have a police escort ready for him. Then he headed off to the hospital and then to the Holiday Inn Express, the same one where Kate had been attacked. He arrogantly dared the assassin to try and attack him there.

THIRTY-SEVEN

"Four cops! This assassin has killed four of our finest and we still do not know anything!" The Chief of Police had called an emergency meeting of the combined FBI-homicide police and he was on a rampage, rightfully so. "Tell me what you have!"

Conrad Toughfston, the FBI lead on the team and the individual who was officially in charge, allowed the Chief to have his rampage. Four of his officers had been killed and an FBI agent had been injured and if the deaths would have been FBI agents it would be Conrad who was on the rampage.

The room was silent so Conrad spoke up, starting his review of the status of the investigation, "What did we learn from the owner of the car that was used?"

"Nothing," replied one of the detectives. "He was at work the entire time. Apparently, the assassin stole his car and used it specifically for the drive-by. We still have the CSI team going through the car but it appears that the assassin wore gloves. There are no identifying marks. We did find some 380 caliber cartridges but they have also proven to be clean."

"How about cameras and videos at the hotel?" asked Conrad.

"The hotel video shows the assassin driving by, but he was wearing a ski mask so we don't have much to help us ID him," commented the CSI lead. "We have pictures of him positioning himself in the parking lot but he seemed to know where the cameras were and we never got a clean picture of the driver."

"Is there anything else that we're working on and that we can share?" asked Conrad.

The CSI detective spoke up again and said, "We also have video from the shopping mall. We can see him getting out of his car and getting into the stolen vehicle that he used to misdirect us. It was at the far end of the parking lot so we could not get sufficient details to get a license plate, but we could get somewhat of a description of the assassin, and we knew what vehicle he was driving. We have several agents out checking the parking lots of the Helena hotels to see if we can spot any cars similar to the one, he was driving and so far, we have found three white Toyota Corollas, but we are not done looking. We are assuming that the assassin is not a local and that he has to stay at a hotel somewhere close by. We are also assuming that he is going to stay in the area until he knows for sure Kate has died, so keeping her alive has a distinct advantage in our search. We believe the assassin may have made his first mistake."

"Incredibly good news," commented Conrad. "Let's put as many resources as necessary into tying down this lead before the assassin gets wise to us and switches cars."

One of the detectives spoke up, "He has been known to park his car in nearby parking lots instead of in the hotel parking lot. That is what he did the last time he hit Kate. We need to look broader than just the hotel parking lots."

"Excellent point," responded the Chief. "I will give you as many men as you need to check out this lead. We need to catch this bugger!"

"Agreed," commented Conrad. "I am going to pull in more FBI resources as well. We need to swamp these parking lots and find these cars, and then we need to track down the owners of the cars. We have a fuzzy picture of the assassin, and even though it is not much, it can be used to eliminate suspects that do not pan out. Let us get out there immediately." Then he turned to the CSI lead, "You already have a plan formulated for these searches. Please incorporate everyone in this room, including myself, if necessary, to do these searches in the hotel and nearby parking lots. And let us find their owners. It may require stakeouts of some of the cars, and that is OK. Please keep me informed and let us report back in about three hours what we have found or where we're at." Then turning back to the group as a whole he said, "Let us do this and get on it quickly. This is the best lead we have ever had on this guy. Let us not let him slip away. And remember that we are doing this for our four fellow officers."

The CSI lead took over and said, "Before anyone leaves this room, I need teams of three, which will allow us to leave someone behind in case we need to do any stakeouts." He organized teams, assigned a pair of hotels to each team, and sent them on their way. Everyone was excited and hyped. They wanted this guy badly.

The teams spread out to the thirty-ish major hotels in the area and the twenty-ish boarding houses. The parking lot searches did not take too long. They targeted white or silver Corollas which were easy to spot and identify. The real work began after one of the vehicles was identified. They would go to the hotel front desk and request a listing of the hotel guests and their vehicles, but most of the hotels had very minimal information about the resident's vehicles. They also took detailed pictures of each of the vehicle's exterior, license plates, and interiors through the vehicle windows.

If a vehicle's owner was identified, then they would take a picture of the owner and his ID, but if the owner were not easily identified, a detective would be left behind doing a stakeout on that vehicle, waiting for the owner to arrive. Once the car and its driver were documented, they released the vehicle and its driver. This documentation process could take hours, but the police were committed to following this search through and not leaving any stone unturned. The assassin was not going to get away this time.

Jill, who had already left the meeting, rushed back into the conference room and yelled, "The hospital! We need to put a team on the hospital. We know for sure he goes there. We need to check all the cars there and continue monitoring it all day in case his car shows up there!"

Conrad responded, "You are completely correct. Why didn't we think of that before? We will send a team out there right away."

It wasn't long before a team was sent to the hospital, and another one of the hotel teams, when they had finished their assignment, was sent directly to the hospital. About an hour later, a third team who had finished their hotel assignments, was also dispatched to the hospital, going completely around the hospital and the nearby doctor's offices, making sure every white Corolla was identified.

The searches went on for the entire day and the teams identified thirty white or silver Toyota Corollas, documenting each of them and doing CSI tests on the vehicle whenever the driver permitted them too, which was almost always. There were only a couple cases where the tests were refused. One was a political activist who resisted anything to do with the establishment, and the other was a known drug dealer who ended up having enough time to clear out any drugs before the warrant arrived. In both cases, warrants were quickly acquired and even those cars were tested. The results were disappointing so far, but they were not giving up. There were still several cars that had not been checked.

Brack looked out of his hotel window toward the parking lot and noticed several police officers swarming around his white Toyota. "Oh rats," was his aloud comment. "I wonder where I screwed up."

He knew he had to take immediate action. He snuck out of the hotel room, went down to the main floor of the hotel, and exited out of a side door, avoiding the lobby and the front entrance. He was on the run. The hotel room and the car had to be abandoned. He had to produce another vehicle, using a different ID, and he did not want to steal it because that would raise another flag for the police to follow up on. They had made quick work of finding the vehicle he had stolen for the hit on Kate. He used his cell phone to locate a Rent-A-Wreck location, booked an Uber to arrive a few blocks away from the hotel, and was soon on his way to getting a replacement vehicle. Once he had rented the car, using another fake ID, he was off to look for a hotel. This time he would use a second-rate hotel, which would have a lower priority in the police's search. He settled in and knew the best thing he could do was to stay underground for a day or two until the police heat died down.

All the hotels were highly cooperative and, when they had a Corolla in their parking lot, they offered up any information and any surveillance camera footage that the police wanted. Everyone wanted to capture this assassin. At the end of the day there were only a couple of cars that had not been identified and documented. Both were traced to car rental companies. One was seriously overdue and the rental company was glad to learn about the location of the vehicle. It turned out that the driver / renter had passed away and no one seemed to know anything about him renting a car. The other was a car that was rented in Idaho. The police quickly made the connection between this driver, and a hotel registration. Then they went to the videos of both the car rental company and the hotel, and they positively identified it as the same person. They staked out the car and the hotel room, hoping that the driver would show up but he never returned to the room or to the car.

Conrad and Jill were in the conference room discussing the progress of their search and he said, "we know who the assassin is. The sketchy image we have of him from the shopping mall matches the images from the hotel and the car rental place. I am convinced we have the right guy, but somehow, he became wise to us and he has again disappeared, avoiding our detection."

Jill tried to give it a positive spin by saying, "We now know more about him than we ever did. We finally have a clear image of him. We know his credit cards and we can track that. We know his cell phone from the hotel register. We need to impound the car and let CSI have access to it and see if we can learn any more from that. We have him on the run, which hopefully means he's going to make more mistakes. As long as we keep Kate alive, at least in the press, he is going to stick around and we are going to get this satanic idiot."

"We're definitely not going to let up on him, that's for sure," commented Conrad. "His ass is ours!"

THIRTY-EIGHT

After leaving the base, Dereck returned to the hospital in order to check on Kate. He found she was still in the ICU hooked up to all sorts of monitors and life sustaining equipment. She looked as bad as the last time he had visited her. He resigned himself to the fact that he was going to be finishing the mole investigation without her help. But more importantly, he was concerned about losing the best investigator he ever worked with. And he was losing a friend. He had all but given up hope for her recovery.

Dereck returned to his hotel with the recordings of the six meetings, along with the two suspicious telephone numbers. His first focus was on the phone transcripts. The first transcript he went through was Captain Viola Grant and he discovered that she was obviously having an affair with someone on the base. The messages focused on when and where they were going to meet and how much they missed each other. However, the message chain from Lieutenant Blanch Taylor's phone was a series of double-talk messages which had a series of coded and encrypted sections that were extremely suspicious.

"Got you!" was Dereck's aloud burst. But he knew he could not convict her because of some weird phone texts. He had to have some concrete evidence. He would set up a trap. He would have to debug her encryption code and follow her to see if there was any type of drop-off point for the messages that she gave out to her contact. He was not sure if the encryption was the entire message that was being shared with a foreign agent, or if the message was just telling her contact that she had information that would be dropped off at their usual drop-off point. Dereck hoped for the latter since that would be traceable and verifiable.

The following morning Dereck was ready. He had prepared tracking equipment that he would attach to Blanch's vehicle, and he had put a notifier on his phone that would beep a specific signal every time Blanch sent or received a message using that encrypted phone. His next step would be to find a techie expert that he could use to debug the encrypted phone texts, but he didn't want to use anyone from the base because he wasn't sure of their loyalty. He decided to contact Jill in the police department. He placed the call and when she answered he asked, "Do you know anyone who is a techie guru who could help me with decoding some encryptions?"

"What are you working on?" asked Jill.

"You know I can't tell you," responded Dereck. "But I can tell you we are close to solving our case and I desperately need a techie genius to help me."

"I have the perfect person," responded Jill. "He works for the police department, and we have become dependent on him, but I am sure he would not mind making a few bucks on the side. Do you want me to connect you with him?"

"Definitely," responded Dereck.

"I'll have to check with him to make sure he wants to do it, but if he says yes, you'll be getting a call from him," said Jill and then she disconnected the call before Dereck could thank her.

About half an hour later Dereck received a call from an unknown number. Hoping it was his techie he answered the call with, "Hello."

"Is this Dereck?" asked Samuel Ledger.

"Yes," he said, being cautious.

"I'm Samuel Ledger from the Helena homicide unit," said Samuel. "I understand you need some techie help. Jill recommended that I talk to you because you have a job for me."

"Can you meet me at my hotel tonight so I can show you what I need help with?" asked Dereck. "The problem is that I need this done quickly and I know you're working on the assassin case so I don't want to distract you from that."

"I'll be there," responded Samuel.

"Six PM at the Holiday Inn Express," added Dereck.

"See you then," replied Samuel.

After arranging what he hoped would solve his encryption problem, Dereck did his usual routine, going first to the hospital to check on Kate, and then going to the base to meet with Conner Brighton. At the hospital he found that there was no change with Kate. It was discouraging and yet he had to continue to have hope. At least she was still alive. He had grown to feel a fatherly form of love for this girl who was a little bit of a rebel, and he now cared deeply about her recovery.

He went on to the base and went directly to Conner's office. At the base he entered the office and immediately asked, "Anything new?"

"No," replied Conner. "What do you think we need to do next?"

"I would like to plant tracking devices on a couple of vehicles, specifically Captain Viola Grant and Lieutenant Blanch Taylor. Dereck did not want to let on that he knew who the mole was because he did not want that information to leak out. "I also want to get any additional phone and email transcripts for both of them that may be more current than the ones Kate already had just to see if anything new has come up. Can I get them printed out so I can go through them in detail? I have what Kate had but I want to see if there is anything new."

"No surprise there," commented Conner. "I'll have that done right away." Then he went on to say, "I was wondering if we catch the mole if that really solves the problem. Isn't there a bigger fish to fry here? Do not we want to get her contact too. Don't we want to catch the big fish?"

"Of course, you're correct," responded Dereck. "However, the other piece of this puzzle is evidence. We cannot accuse someone of being a traitor based on suspicious messages alone. We need to catch them passing information to an unauthorized contact in order to make our case for an accusation of this type."

"So, what we're saying is that, even though we've narrowed it down to a couple individuals, we've still got a long way to go before we can close this investigation," added Conner.

"That's about the size of it," commented Dereck.

"I will get you transcripts. Give me about an hour. And I will put the trackers on the cars as well. It is better if I do it then you cannot be accused of spying on our military employees," replied Conner.

"Thanks."

Dereck went off to the side office and went through some of the transcripts he had previously received, but he did not come up with anything new. After waiting about one hour, Conner came to him with the printouts that he had requested. "The tracking devices are on the cars, as requested," added Conner. "Hopefully this helps track down the location of any drop-offs."

"Thanks," was all Dereck said. Later he added, "I'll head back to the hotel." He was convinced that sitting on the base was not going to gain him anything new. He could watch Blanch Taylor's car from the hotel just as easily as from the base, and he would get less questions that way.

Dereck was about to pack up his computer and head out when he noticed on his tracking software that Blanch was heading for the gate of the base, obviously planning to leave. Dereck went quickly to Conner and mentioned, "Blanch is leaving. I am wondering if she was warned about her car getting tagged?"

"I hope not," responded Conner. He quickly called security and said, "I need immediate support."

"How can we help," asked security.

"I need someone to follow a vehicle. Is that something you can do without being spotted?" asked Conner.

"We'll do our best," responded security.

Conner gave them the details of Blanch's car and added, "Keep me updated on where she goes and what she does. This is top security, and she cannot know she is being followed."

"Understood," responded the chief of security who had now taken over the call.

Lieutenant Blanch Taylor had an office that gave her a view of the parking lot. Occasionally she would look outside to see what the weather was like. She enjoyed an afternoon stroll if it were not raining or windy, and she would go to a nearby park, Spring Meadow Lake State Park, to take a break in her day. This park also happened to be the drop-off point for any information that she would send out. She used a specific garbage bin in which she threw any messages. She would also send an encrypted text letting her contact know that there was something that needed to be picked up.

As she was looking out of her office window, she noticed someone walking behind her car. That did not seem suspicious to her until the individual temporarily disappeared. Then, a few seconds later, the individual reappeared. He had obviously stooped down behind her car. It might have been innocent in that he may have dropped something, but Blanch was in a suspicious mood and was convinced that he had done something to her car, and that was unacceptable.

After about five minutes, Blanch's suspicions got the best of her and she decided that she needed to drive off the base and see if someone was going to follow her. She had to know if someone was suspecting her of being a mole. She left the building, got into her car, and started to drive toward the base's exit. There was the usual line of cars exiting the base, and that was not enough to convince her that she was being followed. Once she was off the base, she drove an unusual route. She drove to a nearby subdivision and circled around some of the streets.

She was convinced that she was being followed. The same car kept reappearing again and again. Now what was she going to do? She streaked off down Euclid Avenue, heading east, at speeds that exceeded the speed limit by thirty to forty miles per hour. She was on the run. She tore through several intersections with red lights, barely missing the cross traffic. It was not long before she had several police cruisers joining in the chase.

The original security officer that was following her from the base, dropped back when she started her dash. He did not want to get into the mix with the police officers. That would just complicate everything. The security police reported what was happening and said they were leaving the chase and the arrest to the local traffic police.

Euclid Avenue became East Lyndale Ave which took a sharp right turn just past Bullman's Wood Fired Pizza. The high speed she was travelling through the city was too fast and it did not allow her to make the turn. She ended up rolling her car down Helena Avenue. The car spun to the left and rolled five times, blowing out every window in her car and crushing down the roof. The airbags, both front and side, had all engaged and had protected Blanch from serious injury, but she did get her neck and back torqued to where she wouldn't be able to walk straight for several weeks.

The police surrounded Blanch's vehicle and, seeing that she was no threat, helped her get out of the vehicle. She was immediately arrested, handcuffed, and placed in the back seat of one of the cruisers while the police worked on cleaning up the mess that she had created.

The mole had been stopped, or had she?

THIRTY-NINE

Conrad, the FBI lead, worked with Jill to set up face recognition equipment throughout areas where they expected the assassin to come, which included the hospital and the major onramps to the freeway. This was an elaborate process, but everyone felt it was critical and necessary. They were willing to throw all the money and resources they had at capturing an assassin who had killed four of their finest, and a half dozen other Helena citizens. No expense was too much at this point. They knew who he was. They even had a couple of his aliases. They were going to get him.

Soon the afternoon news came out. Kate had died. Her lead doctor, Brenda Kidman, had decided that she was never going to recover and had made the decision that it was time. Kate's death was big news because she was connected with the hunt for the drone assassin or drone serial killer, as he was now known. Kate had been the only surviving member of his rampage of murders, and now she too was gone.

Brack Hellringer was thrilled. He saw the news. His assignment was completed and now his primary objective was no longer Kate, but it had become getting out of Helena. And he was going to make his escape that night, in the middle of the night, when there was the least risk of him getting spotted.

Night did not come soon enough for Brack, but he wanted more than darkness, he wanted solitude. He wanted as few people around as possible. At one in the morning, he decided to go for it. He drove out of his hotel and headed for the freeway. He was not aware of the face recognition cameras that had been set up and, as he took eleventh avenue to the freeway, and as he approached the freeway onramp, a camera took his picture. Seconds later Jill and Conrad were both awaken by their cell phones blasting out an urgent message that the face recognition equipment had identified their assassin.

Conrad checked to see what was discovered, and he found that the assassin was heading south down Interstate 15 toward Butte. He also saw the vehicle that the assassin was driving and shared that information with everyone involved in the search. He immediately contacted every police office along that route, including Montana City, Clancy, Jefferson City, Boulder, Basin, and of course Butte. From Butte, the FBI office and the local police all started north on Interstate 15 back towards Helena in the hope of stopping this assassin. Helena also sent a contingent southward.

Fortunately, after getting slightly below Helena, there were very few turn-offs where the assassin would be able to ditch his vehicle and hide. Brack was on a one-way road without an exit.

Conrad calculated the approximate position of the assassin, based on how long he had been travelling, and relayed that information to each of the police units. He was sure they had the killer cornered in. It was just a matter of time before he would be captured.

But Brack had other ideas. He saw the lights of a police cruiser off in the distance coming his way and he was fortunate enough to have an exit coming up. He shut off his headlights and took the Boulder exit. He turned left, turned his headlights back on, and drove up Highway 69 past the Exxon gas station. He pulled off the road, turned his headlights back off, and waited. He watched the three police cruisers blow by the exit at high speed. He waited a little longer and saw two more cruisers blow by. He decided that they must be looking for him. What else would so many police officers be doing in the middle of the night?

He decided to continue on Highway 69 up into the hills above Boulder. Either he was going to have to wait it out or else he was going to continue down the highway hoping that it led to some alternate route that he could use to escape capture. Highway 69 was a slow, windy road and it seemed to take forever for him to get anywhere, but eventually he saw that he was going to end up on Interstate 90, where he would be able to head east toward Bozeman.

The police had a lucky break. One of the residents of Boulder, a retired police officer, liked to keep his radio tuned to the police band, and he was caught up in the excitement of listening to the chase. The police band woke him up in the middle of the night, because of all the intense chatter. It was obviously more than just a traffic stop or even an accident. This was the big time. They were on the trail of a serial killer who had killed officers. It was exciting. He could not sleep. He was up, sitting in his living room, feasting on every word. Then he heard, "We lost him! He must have pulled off somewhere, maybe taken an exit."

Another of the officers, this time an FBI agent, said, "By my calculations, if he got off, it had to be in the Boulder to Basin area. What side roads do we have that he might have used?"

"We'll search those areas," responded a third officer. "We're close to there now."

The retired Boulder resident was looking out of the window, watching as a series of police cruisers flew by on Interstate 15 when he saw something interesting. He saw a car, which had pulled off over to the side of the road, suddenly turn its lights on, pull out, and head south on the highway. At first, he did not think much of it, just some teenagers necking, was his initial thought. But as time went on, he thought more about it and he thought, what if that was the bad guy and I did not do anything about it. I had better let the police know and let them decide what to do.

He jumped on the police band and said, "This is retired officer Crum from Boulder. I saw a car that appeared like it might have been hiding out, pulled over on Highway 69. After the police cruisers blew by on Interstate 15, he turned his lights on, pulled out, and headed down Highway 69. I watched for him and he did not come back so either he stopped somewhere on the highway, or he headed all the way to Interstate 90. I do not know if this is anything you can use, but I thought I had let you know."

The response on the police band came back with, "How long ago did this happen?"

Crum responded, "Fifteen minutes ago."

"Describe the vehicle," asked the police dispatcher.

"It was a 05 Chevy Malibu. It was dark outside but I think it was white or silver."

"Thanks," was the response. "That sounds like it might be the vehicle that our assassin was driving when he left Helena. We will check it out." Then the police chatter sent a couple of cruisers down from Boulder on Highway 69. Cruisers were also dispatched from Whitehall to go up Highway 69.

The chase was back on. By this time Brack had made it all the way to the frontage road of Interstate 90. There was no onramp where Highway 69 came to Interstate 90, so he was going to have to follow along the frontage road until he came to an onramp, which would be several miles down the road.

The police coming from Whitehall were also on the same frontage road, knowing that in order to go north on Highway 69 they would have to get there from that frontage road. They had not turned on their police lights so, from a distance, there was no way of identifying them as police. In front of them they saw an old Chevy Malibu turn from the highway on to the frontage road.

"I think we've just spotted him," said the lead police car over the police channel. "He just turned onto the frontage road along Interstate 90. It is pretty unusual to see any vehicles along this backroad, especially in the middle of the night, and especially if it is not a pickup. So, we are pretty sure this is him. What do you want us to do?"

The FBI agent jumped into the conversation and said, "This is a known killer. Do not confront him. Follow him and keep tabs on him. We will send our SWAT team and our FBI team up from Bozeman. I know that is a long way away, but it is best to let them handle this situation. That is what they are trained for. Stay way back and just keep us posted where he is at and if he does anything unusual, like takes an exit."

"Understood," responded the officer. "It is good you are holding us back because we'd like nothing more than to take this guy out after what he's done to shoot up Helena. I would not mind having a few minutes alone with him."

"Keep your distance so he does not get suspicious. Let him think he is safe. We will have a surprise waiting for him once our team is ready," instructed the FBI agent, Conrad.

"Roger that," was the officer's response.

But Brack was not a fool either. He could smell a trap coming.

FORTY

Samuel Ledger, the local police's techie genius who had been hired by Dereck Hardness to decode some encrypted messages, met Dereck in his hotel room. Dereck showed him the messages and explained, "I need to understand what these messages are saying. What we are dealing with here is national security top secret, and I am trusting you to keep it secret. I assume you are trustworthy since you are a member of the local police force."

"Absolutely," responded Sam. "I have no interest in the message. My interest is in the technical side of getting access to the message, and that is what I will be focusing on. I will figure out the encryption code and then turn it over to you to do the full encryption, if you like."

"Let's start with that, but I may ask you to do the full thing if I get too busy," responded Dereck. Dereck still had his day job to do, which was the management of all the different projects that his various employees were working on.

"I'll take this with me and keep you posted on my progress," responded Samuel. "I have software tools on my home systems, which will help me figure this out and they would make it a lot easier to solve."

"Good enough," responded Dereck. "Please put a high priority on it."

"Will do," responded Samuel and he departed from Dereck's hotel room.

Samuel returned home and immediately went to work. Hilda, who was now his live-in roommate, was also there and, without letting Dereck know, Samuel included her in the decryption effort. The two had fun working together, and this was exactly the type of thing that they both enjoyed working on so it was only reasonable to include her in the effort.

It did not take long for them to solve the coding. At eleven in the evening Samuel texted Dereck and informed him that he had solved the messaging and asked, "Should I bring it over to you right now?"

"Definitely," was the response from an excited Dereck. He was amazed that the work had been completed so quickly.

Upon arriving at the hotel, Samuel gave the information to Dereck and explained, "I went ahead and decoded the entire message stream. It was just easier to do while I had the decryption software up and running. I hope you do not mind. Honestly, even after the decryption, I still was not sure what they were talking about."

"Thanks so much," responded Dereck.

"One thing of interest is that there are several streams of messages," explained Samuel. "On stream seems to be to a partner. Another to someone this person is doing business with. And a third one is a group stream to several people at once. I am not sure what to make of the whole thing."

"Thanks so much," responded Dereck. "I'll take it from here."

Samuel departed and Dereck started reading through the messages that had been decoded. He started with the one that Samuel had labelled, Partner. At first it was boring. It did not sound like anything out of line. But then there was an apparent slip up and the message angrily referred to the partner that they were messaging. It was Dick. This caused Dick, in the following message, to give Blanch a severe reprimand where he told her to never use names again.

This also caused Dereck to push back his chair and wonder. Kate had mentioned that she was spending time with someone named Dick on Friday and Saturday nights. Was it possible that this was the same person? The name Dick was very common, especially in Montana, and it could possibly be a coincidence, but Dereck had found, over many years of experience, that far too often coincidences weren't coincidences. He was going to have to check out that angle.

He continued reading through the decrypted transcript and soon discovered that Dick, whoever he was, was the lead and that he was the one giving instructions to Blanch. Dick was some kind of middleman, going between Blanch who was the source of the information, and someone who was buying the information. Dick was somewhat irrelevant, but he held onto his position because the financial payback was really good.

After going through the transcript between Blanch and Dick, he turned to a second transcript which was between Blanch and some unknown individual. Dereck soon discovered that Blanch was working not only for Dick, but also for someone else. She was actually spying for multiple individuals, and possibly receiving duplicate payouts for the same piece of information. This added confusion to the mix. Which of Blanch's customers was the one sending information to North Korea? But then again, maybe it didn't matter. What mattered was that Dick needed to be stopped. Unfortunately, this mole hunt was becoming more confusing by the minute.

The transcript between Blanch and some unknown individual discussed a drop off point in a nearby park. Other than that, there was not much in the communication that helped Dereck's investigation, so he moved on to the third transcript, which was a group communication. It did not take long for Dereck to realize that this communication was a solicitation by Blanch to get other customers. She would throw out feelers, trying to entice someone / anyone to take advantage of her services. She wasn't satisfied in being an agent to only two foreign powers, she wanted even more customers, so she could sell the same piece of information to as many individuals as possible.

Dereck leaned back in his chair and said, out loud, "This lady is a real jewel. How can anyone be so deceptive and at the same time arrogant that she would risk exposure in several different directions. It is incredible."

Dereck decided that he was going to share his information with Conner Brighton, the Base Operations Commander that had been working with him. He would share what he knew about Blanch so that Conner could take over the prosecution of Blanch and make sure she was not inadvertently released by the local police because of a lack of evidence. He did not want her out on bail because she would surely run. He wanted her to remain in custody, either by the local police or by the military police while he continued working on identifying Dick and the other unidentified person that Blanch was working with. To accomplish that he decided to open communication with a cloned phone and talk to both individuals.

Since he had spent most of the night awake, studying the transcripts, he slept in the following morning. At ten he left the hotel and headed to the base. He met with Conner, gave him a copy of the encrypted and decrypted transcripts, and highlighted his findings. Conner was thoroughly impressed and commented, "That is incredible. We had our suspicions about her after yesterday's car chase, but now you are giving me the evidence I need in order to charge and convict her of treason. Thanks for the help."

Dereck responded, "I am not done yet. From these transcripts I have some hints as to who she was passing the information to, and I am going to follow up on those leads. I want to nail her contacts as well. I will keep working on that and keep you informed about anything I find out."

"Is there anything I can do to help?" asked Conner.

"Not at this time," replied Dereck. "I will let you know if there is anything I need your help with. I am going to set some traps and see what happens. You can help by making sure none of this hits the media so no one gets spooked. And keep Blanch in custody so she does not escape our grasp."

"Understood and I'll do my best," responded Conner.

With that Dereck left Conner's office and departed the base, heading back to his hotel where he would devise and execute his traps on Blanch's contacts. It was the type of thing he loved doing. He enjoyed solving mysteries of this type. And he was excited to push ahead with his plan.

Once back in the hotel he sent an encrypted message to Dick and the mystery contact asking each of them if they received the latest information. They both came back and said they had not received anything, so he sent another message to each of them informing them that she is being followed and that they need to give her a new drop-off location. Each of them readily complied, not realizing that she was still in jail.

With the two locations defined, Dereck set up a phony message he printed out on the hotel's business office printer, put the message into an envelope, and headed out to do the drop-offs. He was going to do them one at a time because he could then watch to see who picked up the message. He also printed out a picture of the Dick that played in the band, just in case it turned out to be the same guy.

The drop-offs were complicated by the presence of his police guards. He explained to them what he was doing and asked them to lay back while he was going through the exercise. They could keep an eye on him, but had to stay at a distance, hidden from the drop-off point.

Dereck did the Dick drop-off and then sent him a message that something had been delivered. Then he found himself a hiding place and waited. It would be several hours before anyone arrived to pick up the letter with the message. When someone finally showed up, Dereck started snapping pictures. He had nailed the suspect. But it was not his job to do an arrest. That was the job of the military security forces in conjunction with the FBI.

After Dick left, Dereck zoomed in on one of pictures and, to his surprise, it was indeed the same Dick that belonged to the band that Kate visited. Dereck said to himself, it is a good thing Kate is not around. If she knew that this guy was hustling her for information and to keep tabs on her, she would be after his blood, and I feel sorry for anybody she goes after with a vengeance." Then after a few seconds he had another thought, "It all makes sense. Kate was saying that Dick was a perfect gentleman in that he did not make any advances on her. Apparently, he didn't want to lose her trust for a little booty. He was more interested in getting close to her and learning what she was up to. Kate was starting to wonder if he just was not attracted to her, but it was more than that. Whether he was interested in her or not, he was not going to blow his cover by letting her think she was just a one-night-stand.

With the first mole contact in the bag, Dereck proceeded to go after the second. He followed the same procedure. He did the drop-off of the letter and then went into hiding. But this one would not be quite as easy. The contact had received a message from his network that Blanch was in jail and decided to check up on her status. He discovered that she was still in jail, so he knew this would be a trap. He had watched the drop-off point and had seen Dereck do the drop-off. It obviously was not Blanch doing the drop-off. He watched for a while longer but saw no one else around. He also saw where Dereck had hidden himself and he now knew who it was that was after him. He left without picking up the message that was dropped off. He knew it would be a fake anyway. Dereck's master plan for catching the second of Blanch's contacts had miserably failed.

FORTY-ONE

Conrad Toughfston, the FBI lead, was ecstatic. He felt that now, more than ever before, he was finally going to get this guy. He and Jill, the local homicide lead detective, had reconvened back at the police conference room where the monitoring equipment was higher quality. They were watching and guiding everything as it unfolded.

The freeway was cleared of eastbound traffic by diverting all traffic off in Belgrade to a side-road while the police waited for the arrival of the assassin's car. No cars were allowed to enter the freeway in either direction, keeping the section of the Interstate free of traffic in case a gun battle ensued.

The stage was set. When the cruiser following Brack's car indicated that Brack was getting close to Belgrade, the razor strip was laid across the interstate, and police were positioned on either side behind the shelter of their police vehicles. Suddenly, a silver 07 Chevy Malibu blew through the Belgrade area. The Chevy hit the tack strip at 85 miles per hour, blowing out all four tires and causing the car to careen badly to the side as it slid sideways and then flipped over twice. SWAT police with full vests and automatic rifles rushed in and surrounded the vehicle. The driver had been knocked unconscious, but the airbags had saved his life. They pulled him out of the vehicle, handcuffed him, and carried him to a police cruiser where they rushed him off to be checked out at a nearby hospital.

The SWAT police took a picture of their captive and sent it out to everyone, claiming, "We have him. He is unconscious, but we are having him checked out at the hospital and then we're bringing him in."

Jill and Conrad were thrilled, at least until they saw the picture of an older, heavily bearded individual. Conrad immediately went to the police communications radio and announced, "You have captured the wrong guy. This is not our guy. Send me a picture of the car and its license so I can confirm the vehicle."

A picture of the car was sent out and Conrad confirmed, "This is the wrong vehicle. It is the right brand of car, but the wrong year, and the license plate is wrong."

Just then a communication came out from the cruiser that was following Brack which said, "He has just exited in Belgrade on Airway Blvd. I do not know who you have captured, but the guy we're following is now heading south down Alaska Road."

A barrage of cusswords could be heard over the police scanner, which was uncharacteristic of police communications, but which was understandable under the circumstances.

Conrad directed, "Do not lose him. Let us know if he stops anywhere."

The message came back, "Apparently, he's making a gas stop. It normally would be a good time to nail the guy except that there is a large number of people around. What should I do?"

Conrad directed, "Stay out of site and keep an eye on him while we get the SWAT team back into position. I am going to assume that he is going to return to the freeway and that our trap is still an effective one. Let us know the minute he leaves the gas station and confirm that he is returning to the freeway. Also, I want a small contingent of SWAT to go over to the gas station and be ready in case he chooses not to return to the freeway. Is there a way you can circle around without him seeing you and find a position south of the gas station?"

"Understood," was the response from both the SWAT team and from the cruiser following the assassin.

A few minutes later, Brack returned to his vehicle, and he was off. As he started heading back toward the freeway, he spotted the police cruiser that had been following him parked on the side of the road and he immediately made the connection that he had been found. He quickly flipped around and started heading south.

"He spotted us and he's heading south," yelled a frantic officer into the radio. "He's going south on Alaska Road."

The SWAT team responded, "We are coming on East Cameron Bridge Road and we are about to turn right on Alaska Road. We will try to cut him off. Let us know if he makes any turns."

The radio went silent. The intensity of the situation left all channels open for any communication between the officers following the assassin, and the SWAT officers coming from the south. Sadly, there was not the opportunity to clear the path in front of the assassin thereby preventing any collateral damage or injuries. They simply were not going to give this guy another chance to slip through their fingers and safety was starting to become secondary.

Suddenly the SWAT team saw him coming, racing towards them. They turned their van sideways on the street, daring him to hit them. But he did not hit them. Instead in desperation he turned right onto Gold Miner Lane. Not realizing that this street had no exit. He was stuck.

Once Brack realized his predicament he turned his vehicle sideways on the street and waited for the SWAT team's arrival. He had his hunting rifle ready. He had finally made a mistake from which he was unlikely to recover. He crouched down behind the front of the car, where he was offered the most protection because of the vehicle's engine, aimed his rifle, and fired several rounds at the SWAT vehicle. The high-powered rifle shattered the bulletproof windshield of the vehicle.

The SWAT van came to a stop and several SWAT marksmen climbed out of the back of the van, taking up positions on either side of the van. A war ensued between the assassin and the SWAT team, both sides making a mess of the other's vehicles, but so far no one getting seriously injured. The shooting went on for about ten minutes.

The police cruiser that had been following the assassin pulled around Motherlode Lane which was the other end of a U-loop road. They followed this around until they came to the opposite end of Gold Miner Lane, and behind the assassin. Unfortunately for Brack, he did not realize that there was now a police cruiser coming up behind him.

"We're behind him," said the officer on the radio. "We are to the side so we are out of the line of fire for the SWAT team. Can we shoot him?"

Conrad exclaimed, "Stay back. The SWAT team may overshoot their target and you would end up getting hit, and that would be an unnecessary tragedy so stay out of their line of fire."

There were so many shots being fired by SWAT and by the assassin that over the radio it was difficult to tell who was shooting. But then there was a unique sound that could readily be recognized by everyone as a shotgun going off. And then everything went quiet.

After a moment of silence Conrad asked, "What just happened? Why did the shooting stop?"

"We heard a shotgun go off which caught us by surprise, and it wasn't our target who did the shooting," responded the SWAT lead. "We stopped shooting to see what had just happened."

"So, what's the status with our assassin?"

"It's too late," said the lead SWAT officer. "It looks like one of your local police officers came up behind him and to the side so he was not in line with SWAT shooters. He blasted him with a shotgun to the head. I do not know if he is dead. He is down. We are checking to make sure he is down for good."

Moments later the lead SWAT officer came back, "One of the local boys got him good! He is definitely down and will not be getting back up!""

Conrad requested, "Send me his picture. I want to confirm that we got the right guy this time. And send a picture of the front of his vehicle including his license plate."

"Will do," responded the SWAT officer.

Moments later the picture was sent over the police telephone band and Conrad confirmed, "That is our man and that is definitely his vehicle. We have finally nailed the drone serial killer. Congratulations to all of you."

But Brack was not dead. He was badly injured. The shotgun blast had hit his head but had primarily penetrated his back and spine and had left him paralyzed from the neck down.

Once Brack had recovered enough to leave the hospital and return to a jail cell, he stayed there about seven days after which they found him hanging in his jail cell. It was written off as a suicide, but the mystery remains, and has never been explained, *how does a paralyzed man hang himself?!*

FORTY-TWO

Dereck was frustrated. He had nailed one of the contacts, but the other had eluded him. The second contact never showed up, which probably meant that he knew it was a trap. The following morning Dereck went to the base and informed Conner Brighton he had identified one of the contacts, but the second one was slipperier than he expected. Conner commented, "I am thrilled we have the mole in custody, and you have identified who one of her contacts was. We will take it from here on both of them. Let me know if you make any progress on the second contact."

"I'll keep you posted about my progress," responded Dereck.

Dereck returned to the hotel and decided that his next move was going to be to triangulate the location of the second contact's phone. He was going to try to identify him or her based on the location of the phone. He only hoped his target had not thought to turn off their phone.

Dereck had a lucky break. The contact's phone was still active and he was able to triangulate the location of the contact. He was at the local Costco. "He must have needed to do some shopping," said Dereck to himself out loud. He left the hotel. His police escort had been reduced to one individual after the news was out that the drone killer had been captured. And he would probably lose that escort as well in another day. They were just being excessively cautious.

He drove to Costco with his police companion next to him and told the escort what he was doing. The police escort agreed to wait in the car, making Dereck look less suspicious without a cop in uniform next to him. Dereck took his phone, started the video player, and positioned the phone in his shirt pocket so that the camera was just over the top of the pocket and was able to record everything he saw and spoke.

Dereck walked the front aisles of the store. His triangulation could only tell him that the phone was in the store but was not specific enough to tell him where in the store. Using a second phone he sent a message to the contact asking him if he was able to pick up the materials that were dropped off. Dereck watched to see if there was anyone whose phone beeped and then they would look at their phone. The problem for Dereck was that several people's phones beeped, and he had no idea if any of them was the phone of the individual he was looking for.

Then it happened. One of the individuals whose phones had beeped because a message was received, stepped out of the checkout line, leaving his shopping cart behind, and started rushing toward the exit. Dereck was not certain that this was the individual he was looking for, but the behavior seemed suspicious. What made him even more suspicious was that the individual looked familiar; like it was someone he had seen before and that he should recognize.

Dereck quickly started heading for the exit, following the suspicious individual. He simultaneously placed a call to the officer that was his escort and explained, "There is a woman rushing out of the store wearing a red coat. Can you keep an eye on her and if possible, get a description of the vehicle and its license plate? Pictures would be great."

"I will do my best. I see her coming out of the store right now," explained the officer. "I'll watch to see where she goes."

"If you have the ability to follow her, please do it. I will get an uber and meet you back at the hotel later this evening."

"Will do," responded the officer.

Unfortunately, the officer was driving a police cruiser which made him stand out like a sore thumb. Brenda got into her car and started to exit the parking lot and the officer was not far behind in his cruiser. But Brenda was not a dummy and she knew that there was the possibility that the officer was tailing her so she made several manipulative and unnecessary turns through a local subdivision, watching to see if she had lost him.

Her antics did not lose the officer and at one point she made the mistake of turning onto a dead-end street. The officer was still following her but was far enough behind her that she had a few minutes to prepare. Now she was in a panic. She climbed out of her vehicle, taking her 380 Auto pistol with her, and she went behind a bush on the side of the road.

The unfortunate officer drove up behind her, stopped his vehicle, and climbed out in order to investigate. That turned out to be his final and fatal mistake. She was waiting for him. In her panic she did not shoot him once but emptied all eight rounds of her semi-automatic pistol into the officer before he even had the chance of pulling out his own weapon. Then she jumped into her vehicle, spun it around, and headed off, hoping she had eliminated her threat.

She headed for the freeway. Unfortunately, she had made the mistake of not realizing that the police cruiser had a forward-facing camera, which recorded her vehicle and saw her climbing into the vehicle. She was on tape racing away from the murder scene. Her cover had been blown and she realized it as she drove away.

Police arrived on the scene of the murder within minutes after the crime had been committed. The neighbors in the area had heard the gunshots and had called 9-1-1. The police quickly reviewed the car's video and were able to identify the car and its driver. Police went to her home but found that she was not there.

Fortunately, the face recognition equipment which had been set up on the freeway onramps and offramps was still active and Brenda's face was used for tracking. It was only a few minutes later when they saw her jumping on the freeway, northbound. "She's heading for Canada," Jill, the lead homicide detective said. "Let's make sure she never gets there."

The police in Great Falls were informed and they were immediately dispatched, heading south on Interstate 15. A local policeman from the city of Wolf Creek was positioned at the only possible alternative route that she might take, which would be on Highway 287 toward Augusta. He was told not to engage. His instructions were to watch and report which direction she went.

A few minutes later a message came out over the police band which said, "She just blew through here at about ninety miles per hour. She did not take the 287 cut across. She is heading north on 15. I hope you guys from Great Falls can stop her. She is a cop killer."

"No worry," came back the Great Falls cops. "We'll get her."

The Great Falls cops knew Cascade, a small town with only one street running through it, was the only exit she could take between Wolf Creek and Great Falls, but they hedged their bets that she would not do that. They were counting on her blowing past Cascade and continuing on to Great Falls. The police officers had circled around to the northbound lane and had hidden behind some trees on the side of the freeway. They were ready to pounce.

They had made the correct decision. Brenda was too flustered to think straight, and she was of the mindset that they were still working on the crime scene back in Helena. She had one objective which was to get to the Canadian border.

When she blew by the area where the police were hiding, the cops rushed out to meet her. Before she realized what was happening, she had cop cars on either side of her, in front of her, and behind her, and they were slowing her down. She grabbed her pistol, aimed it at the cop in the car on the left side of her, and pulled the trigger. Nothing happened. Then she realized her mistake. She had emptied the cartridge out on the cop in Helena. She was in a panic and had forgotten to reload. It was not like in the movies where guns never seemed to run out of ammunition. Her gun was empty. She did the only thing she could do. She stopped her vehicle, climbed out, and put her hands up in the air.

The cop from the car that she had tried to shoot came over to her, spun her around, and slammed her against her car. Then he said, “You tried to kill me, didn’t you!”

She said nothing.

He handcuffed her, walked her over to his vehicle and, in helping her into the back seat, he “accidently” banged her head against the frame of the car door as he was pushing her into the vehicle. To say he was angry would be an understatement.

The message went out on the police band, “We got her. Unfortunately, we will have to book her in Great Falls, but you guys from Helena can pick her up anytime tomorrow. We may end up pressing charges against her as well since she tried to shoot one of our police officers, but fortunately her gun was empty. If you get your murder conviction, then we will be satisfied.”

“Thank you, Great Falls,” was the message Jill sent out.

Dick was not home when the military security forces, in partnership with the FBI, visited his home. A guard was posted outside his house and they waited around most of the day, but Dick never appeared. They also went to the university where he worked. Again, that was a waste of time. Dick was nowhere to be found.

Evening was approaching, and Dereck had mentioned to his contact on the base that Dick was part of a cowboy band. It did not take too much effort for them to find out which band he was a part of. Their next stop was to the cowboy bar where Dick would be playing. This time they were in luck. Dick would avoid his home and he would avoid his work, but he would not cut out on his band gig.

The FBI came storming onto the bar in full force and raced toward Dick. When he saw them coming, he decided to run for it, heading out the back door of the bar, only to find even more agents waiting for him there. He uselessly pled his innocence, but it did not matter. The FBI and the military police had the video evidence that Dereck had provided and they knew that Dick was on his way to a long vacation in prison.

FORTY-THREE

Dereck met with his base contacts the following morning. First, he met with Conner Brighton, the Base Operations Commander, and he told him, "The second contact for our mole was Brenda Kidman, the lady that killed my escort police officer yesterday."

"That explains a lot," commented Conner.

"What blows me away was that she was the one who did the surgeries on Kate, and she was the one that made the decision to pull the plug on her," explained Dereck. "It leaves me wondering if she orchestrated Kate's death."

"That wouldn't surprise me one bit," responded Conner. "Now that we know it was her, it makes things easier for us. She is a cop killer and she will have the book thrown at her for that. We won't even have to arrest her and prosecute her for treason, but we'll do it just to send a message to anyone else who gets any stupid ideas. She will be set for life after those two court cases."

"I feel that my work here is finished," said Dereck. "You have your mole and her contacts. Is there anything else I can do for you?"

"Yes," responded Conner. "You need to present your report to our commander and his VC. I will contact him now and see if he is available."

"Please do," responded Dereck.

One hour later Dereck and Conner found themselves in the commander's office along with the VC. Dereck went through the details of the investigation and explained his findings. Then the commander said, "So there really was a mole on our little base here. I was convinced it was all a false rumor. I need to apologize for being so rude to you and I need to thank you for your efforts and for your results." The commander was still a little nervous about being exposed about his affair with the VC, so he thought he had better play it cool.

Dereck knew what was really happening and just said, "Thank you for your time and let me know if I can ever be a help to you in any other way."

With that Dereck stood up and left the three of them sitting in the commandeers office. His job was finished, but at a great cost, having lost Kate.

THE END

ABOUT THE AUTHOR

Gerhard Plenert

Gerhard, a fervent explorer of fantastical realms, stands as an internationally acclaimed author. His literary journey has led him to craft and publish books for esteemed organizations such as the United Nations, as well as for universities spanning the United States, Japan, and Europe. Remarkably, this upcoming work will mark over thirty published titles—a testament to his prolific creativity.

Beyond the realm of books, Gerhard's quill dances across the pages of journals and magazines worldwide. Over 150 articles bear his name, each offering insights and narratives that resonate across borders. His written endeavors have garnered endorsements from notable entities like Black and Decker, AT&T, and FedEx. Moreover, the esteemed Stephen R. Covey, a bestselling author of international acclaim, has lent his endorsement to Gerhard's literary endeavors.

As a globetrotter, Gerhard traverses continents, bridging cultures and industries. His expertise extends beyond the written word; he also serves as a seasoned business consultant.

Facebook
https://www.facebook.com/authorgerhardplenert

LinkedIn
www.linkedin.com/pub/gerhard-plenert/1/b0/75b

Twitter
https://twitter.com/GPlenert

WordPress Blog
http://gerhard338.wordpress.com

Websites
www.donnaink.shop
www.gerhardplenertbooks.com

GIFTS AND EXPRESSIONS

Plenert Creations

Gerhard Plenert's,
"Montana Bleeds"
www.donnaink.com

MONTANA
TERROR
GERHARD PLENERT
A MONTANA RISING NOVEL
MONTANA
TERROR
GERHARD PLENERT
Gerhard Plenert - Montana Rising Series Volume 3

Montana Rising Series
Dr. Gerhard Plenert

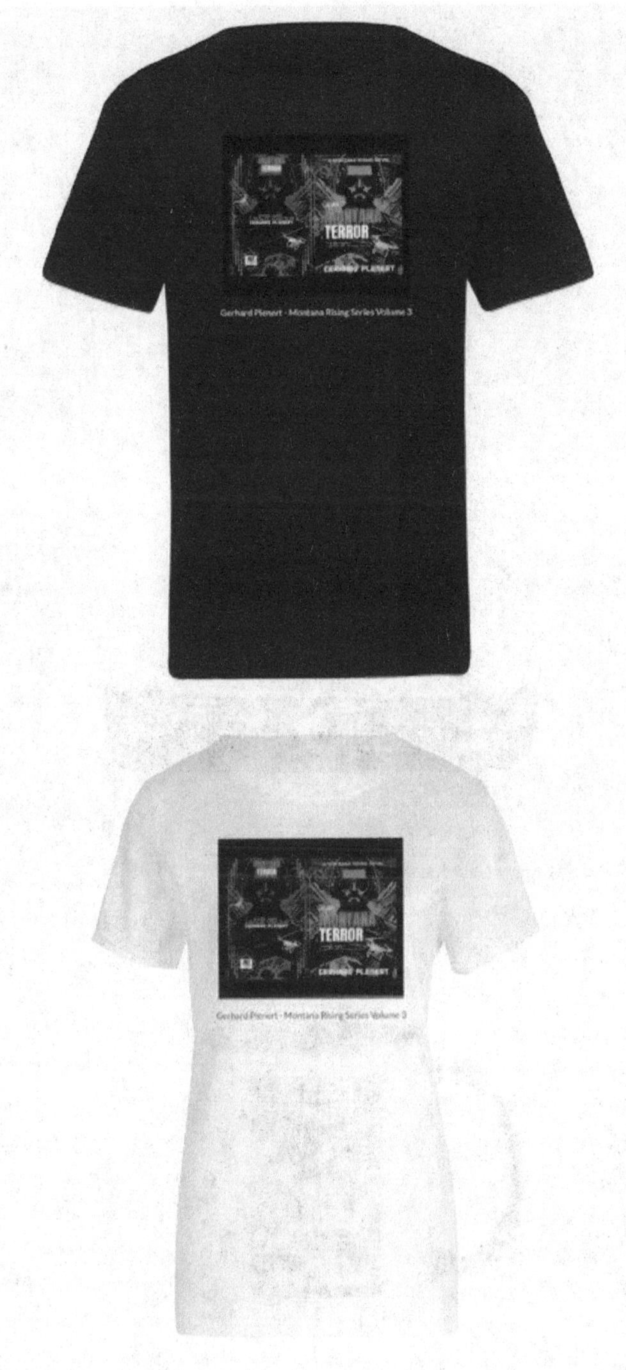
TERROR
Gerhard Plenert - Montana Rising Series Volume 3
TERROR
Gerhard Plenert - Montana Rising Series Volume 3

Gifts and Expressions

Nocturnum's
Muse

Nocturnum's Muse Imprint
DonnaInk Publications. L.L.C.

1390 Chain Bridge Road
#10029
McLean, VA 22101

17811 Aquasco Road
Brandywine, MD 20613
(910) 528-4347
www.donnaink.shop

dpInk
DonnaInk Publications, L.L.C.

www.ingramcontent.com/pod-product-compliance
Lightning Source LLC
LaVergne TN
LVHW031924090820
845145LV00018B/2827

* 9 7 8 1 9 6 0 4 3 1 3 8 7 *